# Bronco's Rough Ride

Siobhan Muir

ISBN: 0692707832
ISBN-13: 978-0692707838

# DEDICATION

Dedicated to all the men and woman who serve in our law enforcement. Thank you for your service. You see the worst of the world and you still try to make a difference.

# ACKNOWLEDGMENTS

Writing a book is never really a one person job. In fact, it takes a great deal of hard work and research on the part of the author to get things correct. And part of that research is talking to people and letting them tell you when you got things wrong. Great thanks go to Silver James who caught my military and police force mistakes, and caught my typos. Thanks to Charley Descoteaux for reading through this tale and finding the logical sticky spots. Thanks to Karla Doyle for being my Typo Sniper, and reminding me to stop grimacing. Hey, I do that a lot, Karla! And as always, thanks to Cara Michaels for designing the most glorious cover art.

# CHAPTER ONE

Chief Petty Officer John "Bronco" Andrews grinned at the waitresses in the tiny skirts as they sauntered past him. Las Vegas was known for its skimpy costumes on the serving staff, even at this off-Strip casino where he'd found a cheap room. He appreciated the display of feminine flesh as he sipped his beer. Too bad his new duty station wasn't located in Vegas. Of course, the SEALs would never get anything done. They'd be too damn distracted. *That, and Vegas is in the middle of the Mojave Desert. Stupid place to put a naval station.*

He appreciated the travel stop, though, and allowed himself to ogle if not touch. He'd already driven damn near twenty-five hundred miles on his way to Coronado to join Team 9, Bravo Squad, and he just wanted a few hours to enjoy the lack of motion. With only three hundred miles left in his drive and a little less than two weeks left for leave, he could afford to take a break. No one expected him at Coronado until the Monday before Independence Day.

An elegant woman with glossy black hair and Asian features leaned against the bar beside John and waved at the bartender. John scanned her sensual curves and the retro silk stockings with the lines up her leg. *Damn, that's sexy.*

His cock stirred at the thought of where those lines led.

The woman glanced his way and offered him courteous but reserved smile. He nodded and let go of his beer to salute her as the female bartender passed him, knocking over his bottle.

"Oh, jeez! I'm sorry." Chagrin pulled at the corners of her mouth beneath pock-marked cheeks. "I'm so clumsy tonight. Let me get you a fresh one on the house."

"That's okay. I was almost done and I have only time for one, anyway." He waved her away.

"I insist. It's my mistake after all." She reached under the counter for another bottle. "Or are you headed out tonight?" She paused and bit her lower lip, her expression troubled.

"No, I'm here for the night."

"Of course, he is." The Asian woman purred as she leaned closer. "I can make your stay even better."

*Hooker alert.* He eyed her lovely attributes swathed in demure red silk and gave her his best non-committal smile.

"Well, honey, that's a mighty fine offer, but I'm just a poor military boy, and your kind of company, while appreciated, might be a bit much for me." His hand closed around the new glass of beer the bartender handed to him. He raised his eyebrows and she shrugged with a grimace.

"Sorry, old habits of pouring out the bottle."

"It's fine. It's got a decent head on it."

"I give great head." The hooker winked as he drank his beer.

John laughed. "I bet you do, honey. But I still think you should find someone who'd truly appreciate your talents."

She cozied up to him with a knowing smirk. "I bet I could make you appreciate it. Come on. On the house."

That was his first clue something had shifted toward FUBAR. The scents of the beer and her bubblegum perfume overwhelmed his nose and his head swam as if

2

he'd downed a fifth of tequila. She pulled him toward her as he swayed, but he locked his spine and pushed away from the bar.

"I gotta hit the head. Be right back, ladies."
*Something's fuckin' wrong.* He staggered toward the bathrooms at the back of the bar, keeping his focus on a still point to make it. He shoved open the door and gripped the edge of one of the stalls, the room spinning.

"Fuck." *Gotta make it to the toilet and throw up.* Had they slipped something into his beer? He shook his head, but stopped when the world shifted dangerously, and he dropped to his hands and knees.

Disinfectant and old piss hit his nose and he gagged. Anything to make him to vomit the contents of his stomach. Yeah, he'd lose his dinner, but hopefully it'd clear out whatever was causing his disorientation.

Unfortunately, the world spun again and he lost his fight with gravity, slamming his head against the stall wall. His arms buckled and he crashed to the tile floor, his sight graying at the edges. *Can't succumb. Gotta make it come up...* John tried to get up, but none of his muscles responded to his brain signals. His ears started to ring as someone appeared in the last vestiges of his view. The Asian hooker leaned over him with a sympathetic expression.

"Poor baby. You don't know what hit you, do you?" She pulled a syringe out of her clutch purse and squirted some of the liquid out the needle. "Don't worry. You'll find out soon enough." An ugly smirk settled on her lips as she jabbed the needle into his bicep. "You'll pay for all the shitty things you've ever done to women."
*What the hell is she talking about?*

"It's too bad you didn't take me up on my offer to give you head. You'd have at least gotten a little pleasure before we knocked you out." She shrugged as his vision dimmed. "Nighty-night, sweetheart."

\*\*\*\*

John woke to find himself tied to a bed tilted to give him a view of the door. Or to give someone else a view of him. A thick strap wrapped around his chest holding him upright. He tried to jerk free, but his body wouldn't respond. At all. *What the fuck?*

As a highly decorated and experienced SEAL operator, John had honed his body into an efficient and responsive killing machine. But that same body now lay against the table as inert as rag doll. His mind screamed at it to move, to roll, hell, to even wiggle its toes, but the messages went nowhere. He wanted to turn his head, to scan the room around him, but his neck refused to respond.

John inhaled to roar, to scream for someone to help. His lungs expanded and his chest rose, but the muscles of his throat wouldn't tighten to make sound, and the air slid out his nose. *Holy shit, what's wrong with me?*

Panic built in his chest, increasing his heartbeat and tightening his gut. His limbs refused to move and a gut-felt moan issued from his chest. *Dial it back, Andrews. There's gotta be a way outta this. It's just not clear yet.* The pep talk dampened the fear and allowed him to focus on external sensory data. He couldn't feel much, but the grayness had left his vision.

The room, while dim and small, smelled of dusty concrete, and the only sound inside was his breath. *Probably not more than ten by ten feet.* From what he could see the only portal in the room consisted of a steel door with a barred window roughly a foot on each side. The concrete dampened any sound coming from outside and heightened the sounds of his breathing.

*Some sort of cell.* He rolled his eyes. *Ya think, genius?*

The door rattled and muffled voices came from outside. Keys jingled just before the scrape of the lock turning heralded the motion of the door. John slitted his eyes as two women came in, both dressed in casual elegance. The taller, younger-looking of the two grabbed his attention immediately as she scanned the room with implacable serenity. Dark hair woven into an intricate pattern lay on the top of her head and his hands itched to pull it down. Her pale-gray eyes slid over his form and his cock rose in response to her causal perusal.

*What the fuck? That works, but the rest of me doesn't?*

"I'm so glad you finally accepted my invitation to visit, Lady Aislynn. As I said before, it's a great honor to have you here." The older woman's voice held admiration bordering on reverence and a smug smile curled her thin lips.

"I was intrigued by the rumors I'd heard of you changing your marketing strategies." Lady Aislynn paused beside the angled bed and her mouth tightened as her gaze returned to John. "How will you increase outreach?"

"Like you, we have a very specialized clientele, so the more traditional advertising avenues are closed to us." The other woman straightened her spine and strode to John's other side. "But we have our chat and email groups through discreet channels. Of course, word of mouth is the best advertising out there."

Aislynn nodded. "And who is this?"

"This is one of our latest acquisitions."

"Acquisitions?" She raised an elegant eyebrow. "You don't appreciate the male of the species?"

"On the contrary. I highly appreciate them." The older woman leaned close, the cloying scent of her perfume swamping John's nose. "Especially when they're docile and immobile. The best man is bound and silent, am I right?"

Aislynn grunted a non-committal sound and studied John's eyes. She raised a hand and stroked him from his shoulder to his hip. A fresh scent—like flowers and spring—reminded him of Washington DC. Cherry trees in bloom. *Yeah, that's it. Cherry blossoms.* The flowery smell pushed out the cloying perfume and sent blood shooting to his cock. *Her touches don't hurt, either.*

"He's remarkably responsive for being so docile. What have you given him?"

"Ketamine. It allows the genitals to be useful while disengaging the more annoying traits of males—their mouths and their strength." The perfume intruded again and his arousal ebbed. "I see he responds to you pretty well. A hard man is good to find, eh?"

Fury ignited in John's chest and he clenched his hands into fists. Except his hands wouldn't respond and his shoulders lay dormant against the slab. *You sick bitch. When I get out of this I'll kill you.* Unfortunately, she'd stated the problem accurately. He lay powerless against her manipulations. For all his strength and training, he'd become one of the weak he'd worked to defend.

Aislynn met his gaze and a flash of emotion broke her serene façade. Anger and disgust burned in her smoky eyes before sorrow crowded them out. The power of her emotion flooded over him and made him wish he could comfort her in the most primal way possible. He strained against his bonds, but his body lay inert. Only his cock rose in salute to the beautiful woman offering him pity.

Aislynn straightened and a distant smile curled her lips, but her eyes showed nothing. Despite the emptiness, his cock flexed and ached for her touch. When she moved away, he mentally whined with distress, wanting to follow her. *What the hell's wrong with me? This is no time for tears or whining. What happened to my training?*

"He has dog tags, which means he's military. How will you keep them from looking for him, Madame LeBeau?" Aislynn retreated to the door, gesturing for the other woman to open it.

The older woman cackled. "By the time they come

looking, it won't matter. Our products have a limited shelf life, if you will. An unfortunate side effect of the ketamine. And our clientele don't care who he is or wish to end their business of having such men." She tilted her head to look at the tags. "Besides, I think there's something ultimately satisfying knowing you have a soldier to play with and he can do nothing. He'll be enjoyed for his attributes and discarded." Her smile turned ugly. "He has a decent sized cock, don't you think?"

"Such a waste, really. I prefer my males dominated by choice, not by drug." Aislynn sent John one more look of sorrow before following LeBeau out of the cell. "Do you have many customers for this sort of thing?"

"More than you'd believe." Madame LeBeau's smile turned avaricious. "So, can I count on you for an endorsement or sponsorship this year?"

John missed Lady Aislynn's response as the door closed behind the women and only his raging hard-on kept him company. He'd never experienced a sexual response to a woman so fast in his life. *Holy shit.* He'd acted like a teenaged boy looking at his first porn. And worse, he'd wanted to protect Aislynn from her sadness. Bronco mentally shook his head. He didn't even know her and now he had sexual frustration to go with his powerlessness.

*Fuckin' awesome. Blue balls and fury. I'm one lucky sonovabitch.* Frustration at his inability to do anything leaked out his eyes in tears, and for the first time since he'd survived BUD/S training, Bronco wept.

# CHAPTER TWO

"Are you sure you wish that one? So few have been interested in him because he's short and hairy." Madame LeBeau's lips turned down as she scanned the man's docile body. "We thought of shaving him, but there is just so much of it."

Lindsey Jarvis let her gaze rest on the monitors of the bound man and forced her expression to remain serene in her undercover persona of Jenna Black, the Black Widow of Las Vegas. Outrage burned through her veins at the treatment of men in general, but specifically this serviceman from one of the armed forces. *The bitch must have slipped him a real Mickey to bring him down.* Even in modern day 2004, sometimes the oldest tricks worked best for manipulation of the strong.

"I want him. He reminds me of my father." Thank God the man looked nothing like her father. Let the creepy madam think she had daddy issues. "But he's much better built than the old man and I'd like to see how muscles like that feel." That at least was true. Her last boyfriend had had the muscles of a marshmallow.

Of course, the last time she'd had a boyfriend was two years ago, when she'd first started this undercover assignment for the Las Vegas Metro PD. She currently played the part of the "not quite grieving" widow of a doctor who'd died under mysterious circumstances just to get into this room with Madame LeBeau. Two years of deep undercover work took its toll on real life relationships.

"What is his name?"

"You can give him whatever name you wish, Ms. Black. Our products are easily modified for your pleasure."

God, the smile on LeBeau's face soured Lindsey's stomach. "Yes, well, it's easier to keep his attention when you have a name.

"Ah, I see." Madame LeBeau gave her a faint, but knowing smile. "I think we can accommodate you." She glanced down at her computer screen, clicking with the mouse. "His name is John."

"John. Right. That is acceptable."

"He is in top condition, but he has not been with us long. I'm sure you understand why he's so heavily medicated. Until the will is broken, the new ones need to be taught their place."

Lindsey let her gaze rest on the monitors as she swallowed down sour bile. Even after two years she still had a visceral reaction to the idea of this sex ring. Madame LeBeau had set up a system where healthy, robust men would be sedated with Ketamine, a veterinary sedative, and used as sex slaves, or for whatever the wealthy psychotic clientele who came to Madame LeBeau wished.

Lindsey had finally infiltrated the upper echelons of the organization to be allowed a "boy toy" of her own. Madame LeBeau had flashed several images of men sedated and bound to tables for her perusal, but Lindsey's gaze had snagged on the dog tags hanging around this man's neck and her decision had been made.

Lindsey tilted her head and gave a half smile as she returned her gaze to the hideously elegant madam.

"I have some conditions."

The perfectly coifed woman raised an eyebrow. "Oh? Making demands, Ms. Black?"

"Not demands, only requirements for my needs." Lindsey curled her lips into an evil smirk, living up to her persona. "I want no audio recordings. Video is fine, but no audio."

"That is highly unusual. We have to maintain a level of safety for our clients."

"I understand. You'll have the video, and I will want a copy of it afterwards, but no sound. What I say to my toy is for me alone to hear." Lindsey turned her gaze to the sexy man strapped to the padded bench on the monitor and licked her lips, playing up her lascivious character. "And for him."

"I don't think—"

"Please, Madame LeBeau." Lindsey raised her chin and hardened her gaze on the woman. "I've paid handsomely for this privilege and you assured me you could attend to every one of my needs." She kept her voice even with just the hint of steel below it. Money talked with LeBeau not sentiment. "This is my wish and what I'd hoped I paid for."

According to the reports, she'd paid an astronomical sum to get into these cloistered rooms. *Yeah, paid handsomely for a handsome victim who couldn't move or say no. Sick bitch.* Lindsey's gut churned but she smiled faintly to disguise her contempt.

"Very well. We shall grant you your request. But the video stays."

"I'd like a copy of it so I may remember my time here at my leisure."

"Ms. Black, while here you may watch it at any time, but I cannot allow it to leave the premises."

"Madame LeBeau, I'm not asking you for the original or all copies of it, I simply want a personal copy so I can enjoy my time over and over again. I've paid well enough for such an unusual request and if it cannot be granted, I will require a refund and I shall leave immediately." Lindsey picked up her purse and looped it over her shoulder. "Do we have a deal or will I be expecting recompense from you?"

Madame LeBeau stood tall, staring down her Gallic nose at Lindsey, but as one of the few female undercover cops, she'd dealt with far more intimidating men and women on the job. The elegant madam didn't hold a candle. Besides, Lindsey needed the video as evidence to bring this bitch down. She just hoped LeBeau wanted the money more than Lindsey wanted the video.

"Very well. I shall allow one copy to be delivered to your suite when you're done with your acquisition." She gestured toward the door on the other side of the bank of monitors. "Are you ready to inspect your purchase up close?"

Lindsey glanced at the handsome hirsute man bound to the table. Her stomach curdled at the way he'd been drugged and trussed up. His dog tags lay on his chest and scars from real action marred the skin in a few places. The reminder of all he'd paid for made her gorge rise. Lindsey nodded and hoped the furious disgust didn't show on her face as she preceded Madame LeBeau out of the observation room.

*Deep breath now. You can't save them all, but you can save this one and get him to tell you everything you need to bring her down.*

The madam led her to a bank of elevators and stepped into the first car. Once the doors had closed, she inserted a key and pressed an unmarked button on the console. The elevator made a smooth descent and they rode in silence. Lindsey eyed the woman curiously as the car stopped and the doors opened.

"These are our holding cells for prospective buyers to inspect the merchandise up close." LeBeau gestured for

Lindsey to follow her down a dark, concrete hallway. "As you have already chosen, as soon as you've enjoyed your sample, we will have your purchase sent to your suite whenever you desire."

"Do I get to keep my goods in my room or must I return them to you when I'm done for the night?"

"The goods are returned to the holding cells for maintenance and upkeep."

Lindsey did some quick calculations and flattened her mouth in displeasure. "How will I be assured no one else will have access to my purchase?" *Sweet God, I won't let anyone else touch him.*

"We take our customers' property very seriously, Ms. Black. Once you've confirmed your selection, your goods will be marked as taken."

"How long do I have to make my decision?"

"Within twenty-four hours of sampling."

"Excellent." She'd already made her decision.

Madame LeBeau nodded and unlocked the faux bedroom door where the soldier lay.

*I will take you down, bitch, just for harming someone who has already paid his dues.*

"There you are, Ms. Black. I hope you enjoy."

"Thank you, Madame LeBeau. I will."

Lindsey made sure the door shut completely and turned the lock to keep out any of the sickly curious. She took a deep breath and turned her attention to the lovely man tied to the padded table.

Dark hair stretched across his chest, down his belly and surrounded his cock and balls. More hair covered his legs and arms. He was every inch a teddy bear, and she'd always been attracted to cuddly bears. However, this bear owned some very beautiful abdominal muscles and she had the unreasoning urge to stroke.

*Time to get his permission first.*

Lindsey tilted her head and set her purse down,

planning her approach. *No doubt he's furious.* She couldn't blame him as she nodded to her prisoner and strode around him. *I'll free you as soon as I can, I promise.* She made a full circuit before she stopped directly in his line of sight.

"As I understand it, you're really in there, alive and awake and aware. So we're going to play a little game." Lindsey gave him a cool smile. "Despite your incapacitation, I know we can communicate just fine and I want you show me you understand. So here's how this will go. You will blink twice for yes and once for no. Do you understand?"

Lindsey met his gaze and waited. The cool eyes never moved or blinked. She stared hard, noting the golden color of his irises. *Dark haired with golden eyes.* He was every one of her fantasies in the flesh and he couldn't move. *Guess I'm going to have to do what I always dreamed I could. I have to save the hero in distress.* Why couldn't she get rescued once in a while? The sick part about the whole situation stemmed from what she'd learned about military and police men. They often joined the cops or armed forces to protect and serve those less fortunate and weaker than themselves. Her father and uncles had been that way. Now this guy lay at her mercy, unable to break free, unable to use his strength or training to save anyone, much less himself. It had to be eating at him like poison.

"Come now…" Lindsey paused as she thought of the name Madame LeBeau had christened him. "John. Answering won't harm you or give away anything you don't want. I just want to be sure we understand each other." She sidled closer to his left arm.

Great muscles swathed the bones and his large hands showed calluses where he'd held weapons. *Definitely a front line operative.* Scars marred the skin on his ribs and shoulders. Old knife marks and bullet wounds. This man had seen some impressive action at some point.

"So, do you understand me?" She leaned over him

until their gazes met and John blinked twice.

"Excellent." She gave him a satisfied smile even while her gut clenched with disgust. "My name is Mistress Jenna and you're to be mine tonight. If you please me, I might keep you for a while. Do you understand?"

John's eyes closed and opened twice more.

"Very good. Now I'm going to smell you. This will tell me if I've chosen the right man. And believe me, you want to be the right man." She shot him a pointed look. "A man's scent tells a lot about him. How healthy he is, what sorts of foods he eats, how well he takes care of his body." Lindsey paused to scan the lovely furred chest and belly, leading straight to his flaccid, but decent-sized penis. "Although given what I can see at first glance, you've taken very good care of this body."

Removing her shoes and purse, she stepped up to the bench and brought her nose close to his hip, inhaling. They'd cleaned him up and washed his skin. The scents reaching her nose reminded her of vanilla Ponderosa pine bark in the sun, but the after-scent soured as if something tainted his sweat. *Damn drugs. We'll fix that soon, John. I promise.*

She sniffed his belly and up the center of his chest until she came to the dog tags. She paused long enough to read the name and rank. Chief Petty Officer J. H. Andrews. At least she'd have a name to report to her handler. She continued to his neck and bearded jaw, enjoying the brush of his chest hair on her chin. Glancing up, she met his golden gaze burning with fury and inwardly scowled. *I'm sorry.* She wished she could tell him, but she had no way... *Wait.*

Bringing her nose and lips close to his ear, she brushed aside his long hair and made it appear she tasted his neck.

"Chief Petty Officer Andrews, my name is Officer Lindsey Jarvis of the Las Vegas Metro PD." She breathed the words to his ear and hoped he understood. "I've been infiltrating this sex ring for two years and I'm going to do my damnedest to get you out." She pulled back a little and gave him a satisfied smile. "You smell divine. Do you understand?" She hoped he saw the real question in her eyes. *Please know I'm here to help you.*

"John" Andrews blinked twice, some of the anger replaced with surprise.

"Very good." She sauntered around his head, trailing her hand through his hair, and put her nose beside his other ear. "I need permission to touch you to make this look good. I need complete access to your body, including your penis and testicles. Do I have permission to touch you, including kissing, on your torso and legs?"

Holy shit, what was she asking him? She raised her head from his ear and met his gaze. Curiosity burned there. "So, you're a military man, hm? Do you work that body hard, John?" She placed her hand on his right pectoral above his flat nipple and tried not to enjoy the fuzzy heat from his chest as she stared into his eyes. *Please give me permission. I don't want to have to stop.* Stop the game to rescue him, not stop touching him. *Riiiiggghht.*

John blinked twice. *Thank God.*

"Ah yes, I'm sure you do." She smiled, hoping the relief didn't show too much, and dragged her hand over the hard bumps of his abs. Damn, the muscles she'd always enjoyed on the covers of romance novels felt like velvet covered steel. He embodied both hard and soft together.

"Such lovely muscles." Lindsey slid her hand past his hip and over his thigh. The muscles remained still and she hated the drugs running in his system. One of her favorite parts of touching came from her lover's reactions, and John had none. He could only lie there and watch. She hoped he enjoyed it a little, but she suspected his helplessness ruined the experience.

Lindsey paused at his feet and met his gaze as she settled her hands on his ankles. "You're perfect, John. So lean and hard." She stroked his legs from his ankles to his knees and back. "And strong." She moved to the side and used both hands to massage one of his thighs. With restricted movement, the lovely muscle tone would suffer. "Are you a runner, John?" *Build me a persona, John. Let's play this dangerous game.*

She met his gaze and he blinked once. "Not a runner, hmm." She sauntered closer to his chest, resisting the urge to touch his groin as she dragged her fingers over his skin. "Swimmer, maybe?"

John blinked twice. "Ah, yes, a swimmer. I can see it in your lean lines and flat belly. There's something so sexy about a man dripping wet, and contrary to popular belief, your chest hair won't cause too much resistance in the water, will it?" *Come back to the point of this, Jarvis.* Lindsey bent close to him until they faced each other nose to nose.

"Do the drugs allow your body to react to sexual stimulation?" She hoped he'd understand why she asked her whispered question as she waited for him to blink. He looked at her a long time and she held herself still, though her heart thundered.

John blinked twice, and she released the breath she'd been holding. "Please give me an erection, then, Chief Petty Officer. I'm going to make a play for you to be brought to my room after." She smiled as she nuzzled his neck again. "I can get a nullifier to counteract the drug and a plan to get you out, but to convince Madame LeBeau, I need it to look like I can stimulate you. If I can't, she'll give you to someone else." The idea incited a flare of rage in Lindsey's chest and she tried to smother it. What was wrong with her? Feeling possessive over a stranger? But something about this man ignited all her protective instincts and when it came to rescue, she'd step up to the plate. She just hoped she wouldn't embarrass him.

\*\*\*\*

Bronco wished he could ask her to repeat the question. Officer Lindsey Jarvis from the Las Vegas Metro Police Department wanted him to get a hard-on for her? Of all the things he'd been required to do as a SEAL in the US Navy, this had to be the oddest request ever. Not that it would be too difficult with her soft touches, sultry voice, and her exquisite body. Had he seen the woman in a bar, wearing the slinky black dress with a slit up to her ass, he would have made a play for her immediately.

Of course, in his current state, he wouldn't be making a play for anyone until he got out of this situation. It had looked bleak until she'd walked in and told him who she was. Then possibilities had bloomed in his mind faster than he could lock on them. *Must be the fucking drugs.* They befuddled his mind for all they left him conscious. He hadn't forgotten who he was, but the details of how he'd gotten here had fallen into obscurity. As far as he knew, he'd been on leave on his way…somewhere. Now he lay strapped to another bench of some kind, naked, with his body still unresponsive.

"Such a lovely, lovely body." Lindsey stroked down his chest and belly, swirling her fingers in the hair marking the muscles. Plenty of women had enjoyed the contours, but few had given John as much pleasure as Lindsey's deft strokes. "Does this still work, do you think?"

Sweet, tickling pleasure hit John's brain as she reached his groin, caressing his flaccid penis until the blood damn near left his head without coherence. He closed his eyes, and if he could have moaned, he would've let her know the pleasure she gave. It might not have been professional, but he'd never been one to shy away from a role in a mission. Right now he played the sex slave and she needed a hard-on. Normally he could do that in his sleep, but the drugs messed with most of his abilities.

17

He'd never prayed to *get* a hard-on.

"Ah, see, I knew you had strength and virility when I first saw you, John." Lindsey stroked his filling shaft with one hand and slid the other up his belly. "All this hair. Ummm. So sexy and masculine. My poor husband never measured up to this."

She tilted her head as her hand dropped to roll his balls in her fingers. "He was all about the in and out with a quick swig of alcohol to give him courage. I bet you've never been quick about that or needed the drink to get you going."

Damn, this woman might be the first to make him blow his load way too quick. Lady Aislynn had teased him and left him with the worst case of blue balls ever, but she paled beside Lindsey's earthy sensuality. The cop embodied sexy and sultry better than anyone he'd ever met and being a SEAL, women had never been scarce.

"Oh, yes, that's it, John. Over-fill my hand with your manliness." Lindsey's smile made him wish he could move, grab her, and give her as much pleasure as she currently gave him. "So you like it when a woman takes you in hand." She chuckled as she bent over his groin, out of his sight.

*Holy shit, is she gonna suck me?*

His cock flexed and a spurt of precum slickened her grip at the thought. Lindsey moaned a happy little sound and pleasure jolted through John's body, but her lips never touched his cockhead.

"You smell so good, John, like vanilla spice and hot Las Vegas nights." She tightened her grip on his shaft and groaned with pleasure. "My favorite scents. We should make a candle of you so I can light it and remember our time together." She turned her gaze toward him and licked her lips, stroking harder. "I want to remember this."

Candle or no candle, he'd fucking remember Lindsey Jarvis. Licking her lips had shoved his arousal into high gear and the pressure built in his balls, tightening the skin each time her hand brushed over the hairs there. John had no control, not with the drugs in his system, but for once he was off the hook to give his partner pleasure, even if the idea galled him. He'd never been so selfish when it came to sex.

Lindsey turned more toward him until he could see her face and upper chest clearly. Her nipples pushed taut points against the bodice of her dress and her eyes lidded to half-mast. She moaned a little as she stroked him harder and faster, biting her lower lip. John wished he could move, moan, hell even show her his "O" face as his arousal surged to a screaming level. Pleasure swamped his mind and his balls tightened up just before he toppled into ecstasy.

John closed his eyes and sighed as cum shot from his cock, bathing Lindsey's hand in hot cream.

"Oh yes, yes, John. Come for me." She milked him with her hand and stars sparkled behind his closed lids. *Holy shit, this woman is sex in a dress.* He'd never come so hard by only a hand job.

His heart thundered and his breath shuddered in his chest as the euphoria washed across his senses. Considering how immobile he was, she'd given him the best damn orgasm he'd had in weeks.

"Mmm, you taste divine, John. Like vanilla cream."

The husky satisfaction in her voice made him snap his eyes open and his cock flexed as she licked his cum off her palm with long slow swipes of her tongue. *Fuckin' A, did she just lick her hand?* John had never seen a woman appear to enjoy cum so much and the pleasure from her apparent enjoyment warmed his chest.

She licked and savored her entire hand's worth of cum like a tasty treat and offered him a satisfied smile. He still couldn't move, but the scent of her arousal perfumed the room and delight rose in his chest unbidden. *Damn, at least I made her wet.* That was fuckin' sexy.

When she'd finished cleaning her hand, Lindsey patted his thigh and gave him a happy smile.

"Very good, John. I think you'll do nicely." She sauntered to his shoulders and dipped her head beside his as if to kiss him.

*Oh, yes please. I'll take a kiss, ma'am.*

"Thank you, Chief Petty Officer. I'll arrange to have you brought to my suite and we'll get you out of here as soon as possible." Her whispers brushed his ear and some of his pleasure drained away. He was still a prisoner, but she'd managed, with one small hand and some soft moans, to make him forget his circumstances for a few moments.

Lindsey tilted her head to meet his gaze. "You're very good, John. And you're mine from now on. Do you understand?"

He blinked twice and some part of him couldn't be happier belonging to her. *And when I get a chance, I'll show her.*

# CHAPTER THREE

Lindsey spread her legs and bent over one of them, stretching out her quads. Sweat trickled down her back. Even at zero-five-hundred, the Vegas summer temperature simmered at eighty-two degrees and she'd be drenched before she even started to run. She rose and switched to the other leg, waiting for her handler. They'd agreed to meet at Floyd Lamb Park to discuss what she'd found and how she'd get Chief Petty Officer JH Andrews out of Madame LeBeau's sex slavery market.

"Hey, Jenna. Ready to run?"

Lindsey straightened at her cover name and offered a smile to her LVMPD handler Courtney Dabner as she jogged up. Courtney had the body of a supermodel with wiry muscles and long limbs. Lindsey reminded herself to be grateful for her more compact and robust frame, but Courtney's stature remained intimidating.

"Yes, but not too hard today." Lindsey grimaced as she stretched out her side. "I had a late night last night and I need to go slow to work out the kinks."

Courtney gave her a lewd wink. "Kinky night, huh? Okay, we'll just jog then."

They set off on the paved path around the lake as the

sun painted blue shadows on the western faces of the surrounding mountains. Ducks and coots splashed in the wind-ruffled water and a lone heron fished within the reeds along the shoreline. Lindsey loved the park's diverse geography, from sculpted lawns to rough bluffs with fossil-bearing rocks. It covered several acres and made a great place to trade information.

"So, what's going on, Jarvis?" Courtney breathed easily as she ran. "Your message was more cryptic than usual."

Lindsey gathered her intel and breath as she scanned the path ahead. No one else shared the park this early on a random Thursday beyond a man tossing breadcrumbs to the peacocks across the lake.

"Madame LeBeau vetted me and let me into the selection pool." Lindsey choked back her disgust. "She gave me my first 'toy' to play with last night."

"Good news. Did you get access to her electronic files?"

"No, there wasn't time to set the program. Too many folks in the room while I was going through their catalog." God, the idea of men listed as toys for purchase like in the Sears Wish Book curdled her stomach. "But I will get a video copy of the sessions with my man 'to enjoy at my leisure.' The guy I chose is military, Court. And he's definitely seen some action on the front lines somewhere. I gotta get him out of there. I'm sure he can tell you more than I can since he's stuck on the inside. LeBeau has him jacked up on ketamine to keep him docile, but he's aware of everything going on."

Her rage burned through her gut and she had to push some of it into her strides. *He's serving his country, dammit. He shouldn't have to pay more.*

"Got a name? We can check to see who's missing."

Courtney's calm dismantled some of Lindsey's fury. "Chief Petty Officer JH Andrews. We've been calling him

John, but I don't know if that's the right J."

"Navy, got it. Do you know how long he's been in the ring?"

Lindsey shook her head and waited until they ran past another jogger going the opposite direction. The city had started to wake up and the park would be full soon. They jogged for a few minutes in silence.

"Not long. I'd say they picked him up last weekend. They hadn't shaved him by the time I saw him."

Courtney frowned. "They shave the men?"

"Yeah, it's for the media brainwashing. Everyone wants a romance novel cover model these days, and those guys are bare except on their heads."

"Jesus." Courtney's hands tightened into fists. "Okay, I'll check on CPO JH Andrews and let his CO know what's going on. You know they might send someone to come get him."

"Tell them to leave it alone. I got this and I'll get him out. If they storm the walls guns blazing, I'll lose two years' worth of work." Lindsey gritted her teeth. "I can't let that happen."

Courtney nodded. "Right, so what do you need from me?"

"Two things." *Deep breath, Jarvis.* "I need a nullifier for the ketamine. I won't be able to carry this guy out. He's at least two hundred pounds of solid muscle, so he'll need to move a little under his own power."

"Got it. And the second thing?"

"I want out after this. I'm done with deep undercover. The world is getting dark and sickening and I'm losing myself to it." Lindsey shook her head. "I've put in the paperwork for regular detective in the sex crimes unit. I'll finish this mission, but I gotta get back to being myself and not some psychotic bitch bent on hurting men. Especially military men. That's the last straw, Court."

"Roger that." Courtney shared Lindsey's military

background. "I'll let the captain know. And I'll get the lab on a nullifier for ketamine."

"Good. Do it quick. I want to get him out this weekend. Even as in shape as he is, his body can't take more than a couple of weeks of dosing."

"I know."

The last guy's body had been found covered in ants in the middle of the Las Vegas Wash not far from where they ran now. The ME said he'd died of heart failure from a ketamine overdose. *I won't let that happen to John.*

"I'll need the nullifier by Friday morning. Have a safe house ready by that evening if you can. If not, the latest is Saturday." Lindsey slowed down to a walk as they neared the parking lot. "The Man Cave Club is only really busy on those two nights and that's the only way I can sneak him out."

Courtney nodded as she grabbed her ankle behind her thigh. "When I got what you need I'll text you and bring the nullifier to the regular place. What's your exit strategy?"

"Drunk couple headed home for sex." Lindsey shrugged. "I don't expect him to be steady on his feet and if we come out through the club, we'll blend in with the other partiers."

"What about cameras and bouncers?"

"We can duck the cameras and the bouncers will see what they expect." Lindsey stretched out her quads as she scanned the parking lot for anyone who might be close enough to listen. "Just make sure there's a safe house. We'll both need a place to lay low for a few days."

"Will do."

"And Court?"

Her handler met her gaze. "This is the last one of these. I really can't do this anymore. I'm serious."

Courtney nodded. "All right, Jenna. I'll put in the paperwork if you're sure."

"I'm sure." Lindsey had reached saturation and John represented the final straw in this risky game. "So I'll see you back here on Friday morning?"

"No, I can't. Jeremy's got a camping trip with Scouts. Let's meet for coffee instead. My treat." Jeremy was the name of Courtney's cover son and it gave them an excuse to change their meeting location. "Say nine at the Blue Bean?"

"Yes, I think I can be there. Thanks for the run."

Courtney waved and climbed into her car. Lindsey returned to her stretches and closed her eyes. She'd get out of this false life come hell or high water. She'd save her sexy sailor and win her freedom.

In the meantime, she had to pretend to be Jenna Black, wealthy widow and psychotic bitch. *Though I don't hold a candle to LeBeau.* Lindsey did a few more stretches to alleviate the surging anger and unlocked her car. She needed to stop at the cleaners on the way back to her suite and she might as well check on her purchase. She'd be damned before she allowed anyone else to touch John.

Lindsey climbed into the driver's seat of her car with the door open to release the heat of the early summer morning. The cleaners wouldn't be open this early so she had time to run back to her suite and check on John. An odd excitement built in her gut as she pulled her door shut and rolled the windows down. She couldn't decide if the emotion came from spending more time with the handsome Navy chief or from the end of this miserable assignment. Either way, a smile crept across her lips as she headed back into town from the park.

\*\*\*\*

John wished he could sleep. Wished he could be dead to the world during the long hours of nothing with only his involuntary sensations to keep him company. If his balls itched, he had to endure it. He couldn't move, couldn't stretch, couldn't do anything but breathe and look at the ceiling. They'd done a nice job with the concrete. It even held grooves where the mix had molded to the boards for formation. He'd counted thirty-six knots in his ten-by-ten cell. At least on the ceiling. Who knew what the walls showed. He would have liked to know if only to mitigate the boredom.

Time crawled by worse than his BUD/S training in Little Creek and he'd run out of things with which to entertain himself. At least in BUD/S there'd been pain, or exhaustion, or even the other men to distract him. Here he only had his thoughts. He couldn't even masturbate. Or twiddle his thumbs. At least that'd be something.

*Think about Lindsey.*

Bronco had no idea how much time had passed since he'd last seen the lovely cop, but his thoughts drifted to her and settled. Lindsey Jarvis with her fine ass and her skilled hands. Damn, that woman knew how to rub one out and he'd let her do it any time she wanted. He closed his eyes and imagined her smooth fingers wrapped around his shaft. His cock thickened with appreciation and his balls tightened against the base.

He could almost feel her lips slide over the head and her tongue press into the divot below the glans. *Oh, yeah, sweetheart. Suck it.* Slick heat enveloped him as the cool silk of her hair trailed along his thighs. Pressure increased, building his arousal as her head bobbed up and down his length in his mind's eye.

In his head, he moaned as the soft wet sounds of her lips on his shaft reached his ears. The dark cell fell away and he imagined himself lying on a California beach with Lindsey's sun-soaked hair over his lap. His cock flexed and his orgasm burned in his balls as the waves hissed on the shore and the sea birds cried overhead.

Lindsey's silken fingers brushed the hairs at his groin

and John raced for the pinnacle of his release, his heart thundering for the finish. Only the sound of the bolts turning in the door and the squeak of the hinges blew apart his fantasy and he jerked his eyes open. His cock flexed in protest and his breath sawed in his chest as the door swung inward. *Fuck, talk about lousy timing.*

To his surprise, the subject of his fantasy appeared and offered him a sweet smile, her gaze zeroing in on his stiff shaft. Lindsey licked her lips and some of John's earlier arousal returned. If he could've wiggled like a happy puppy, his body would've shimmied in its restraints.

"What have we here?" Lindsey's sultry voice stroked him better than he'd imagined her mouth, and his cock flexed again. "Have you been pleasuring yourself without me, John?"

How the hell did he answer that one? Yes, he'd used his own mind for pleasure, but in his mind it had been her mouth, her fingers. He moaned his frustration and blinked in surprise as the sound became reality. *Holy shit, are the drugs wearing off?*

She approached his bench and her expression showed surprise. "You certainly have worked yourself into a lather. Would you like me to help finish you off?"

*Does it snow in Minnesota?* He blinked twice, groaning at the back of his throat.

She chuckled and leaned over him, the scent of cherry blossoms filling his nose. *She smells like Lady Aislynn. Is that her shampoo?* The fragrance came from every part of her body and he inhaled with delight as she settled against his side.

"Very well, since you've been such a good boy and waited for me so patiently, I'll give you what you need."

Bronco's cock flexed as the tail of her hair draped over her shoulder and brushed his hip. Damn, not as sexy as a full curtain, but still smooth and cool. She'd recently showered and the wet fringes tickled his hot skin. He enjoyed the sensations until her hot mouth wrapped around his shaft and he lost coherence.

The reality of her mouth far outmatched his feeble imagination and John sank into the sweet erotic pleasure. Lindsey moaned a little as she licked around his head, tickling the edge of the glans with the tip of her tongue. His cock flexed and his balls tightened just as they had in his fantasy. Lindsey must have read the script because her hand slid down between his thighs and stroked the sensitive flesh of his sac. His scrotum tightened and his arousal swamped him, threatening to explode.

*Oh, God, yes. Suck me hard, Lindsey.*

She hummed around his cock and swallowed as if she'd heard his request. The vibration against his shaft tripped his triggers and his orgasm tore through him, shooting stars across his vision. Hot shots of cum erupted from his cock and she swallowed them all, stimulating the head more than he thought possible.

John shuddered with the pleasure, wondering how he'd gotten so damn lucky. Lucky to meet Lindsey Jarvis, and unlucky to be unable to move or reciprocate. SEALs were all about getting the job done and done well, but he could only lay there and take what she gave him. He hated his inability to pleasure such a sexy, sultry woman.

"Mmm-mmm, I've said it before, but you're tasty, John." She licked her lips and Bronco wanted to wiggle like a puppy again. What was so damn sexy about a woman enjoying his cum? "I know you came, but did you enjoy it?"

He blinked twice and moaned, the sound actually reaching her ears. They both paused and hope filled Lindsey's expression.

"I heard you this time. Do you think the drugs are wearing off?"

He blinked twice again. At least he hoped that's what it meant. If he could regain the use of his limbs, they could get out of this nightmare in a heartbeat.

Lindsey opened her mouth to say more when the door to the cell opened again and a technician wheeled in a small cart holding medical paraphernalia. *Aw fuck, here it comes. Right on time.* Lindsey's expression shuttered and her fists clenched briefly before her stoic mask slid into place.

"Oh, excuse me, ma'am. I didn't realize you were attending your product." The younger man looked nervous.

*Fuck, I'm not even human anymore.*

"Yes, well, he's mine to enjoy anytime and anywhere, isn't he?" Damn, her voice could crack like a whip when she wanted.

"Yes, ma'am. Sorry, ma'am." The tech ducked his head. "I just need to administer his dosage to keep him functioning as he ought." He busied himself with the syringes on the cart, studiously ignoring Lindsey's piercing gaze.

"I'm curious. How much ketamine do you give them and how often?"

The tech's shoulders tightened. "It really depends on the size of the product, ma'am. But average is about thirty milliliters every two hours."

"And for my toy?"

"This one takes forty-two, ma'am."

Holy shit, forty-two milliliters of drugs went into his system every couple of hours. That'd be enough to sedate a draft horse for at least an hour. What the hell was it doing to his internal organs?

"Forty-two milliliters every two hours? Won't that harm his internal organs?"

"It can, ma'am, over a prolonged time period." The tech's shoulders tightened even more as he reached for John's arm. "But Madame LeBeau made it clear these products have a limited shelf life, didn't she? They don't last forever."

The jab of the syringe reminded John he still had a

body, but he could do nothing to fight and that just pissed him off more. They fucking poisoned him and he couldn't do a damn thing to stop it. Lindsey wore an expression of cold disdain, but anger burned in her eyes.

"Indeed, she did, but that's no reason to mistreat them." She raised her chin. "I require you to decrease the dosage on my toy to thirty milliliters from now on."

"Ma'am, I can't—"

"Don't hand me excuses, mister. I paid for my toy and I want to use him as I see fit." Her voice brooked no argument. "You will decrease the dosage to my specifications for the usage of my product. Is that clear?"

"But he could regain some of his strength, ma'am."

"You have him secured. The straps are rated for dangerous mental patients, are they not?" When the tech nodded, she added, "There, now, we'll be fine. Only thirty milliliters from now on. Do you understand?"

"Yes, ma'am." The tech gathered up his equipment and cart as he prepared to leave.

"Don't try to weasel out of it, young man. I've had enough chemistry to know how to read a syringe."

"Yes, ma'am."

"Good. Thank you. I'd like to keep my toy for as long as I can." She stroked John's arm possessively as the tech dipped his head. He wheeled his cart out of the cell, beating a hasty retreat. She waited until he'd closed the door before whispering to John. "I know it wasn't much, but hopefully the decrease in ketamine will mean a quicker recovery."

Bronco wished he could tell her he understood, but any noises he'd made while she pleasured him had fallen before the new tide of drugs they'd shot into his system. Frustration raged in his chest, but his body showed nothing, and it only spurred his anger.

"Easy, John, I know you're frustrated." Lindsey stroked his chest and arm with her warm fingers. "Just breathe easy for me. This won't go on much longer, I promise." She crouched beside his head and pressed her lips to his temple. "God, have they even bothered to bathe you at all?"

She raised her head to meet his gaze and he blinked once. Her mouth tightened and anger flashed in her beautiful brown eyes as she stood. "Well, that will definitely have to change. I will not tolerate my possessions to be mistreated." Her voice had risen so anyone listening could hear. "I'll make sure you're bathed so you're ready for whenever I want you."

Oh, he'd be ready. He just wished he could fully participate. Damn, he couldn't even move his lips or tongue to feast on her pussy. A pussy hidden beneath the fabric not more than eight inches from his face. He suspected it would be as luscious and tasty as the woman looked. The fragrance of her arousal reached his nose as she walked around his head to his other side. She stroked his head as she knelt again to put her face level with his.

"Listen to me carefully, John. Today is Thursday and the Man Cave Club is only bustling on Fridays and Saturdays. I can't get you out before then." She kissed his other temple. "I'll get you to a safe house where we can talk about what you've experienced and get enough evidence to bring this bitch down."

The slide of her nose against his cheek and ear calmed him while her words generated excitement. He only had to wait two more days at most and he'd be free of this nightmare. *I can do anything for two days.*

"I'll also have a nullifier to help with the ketamine in your system. With the lower dosage, I'm hoping it will act faster than usual." She slid her hand over his chest and played with his nipples, her motions casual. "I won't be able to carry you, so you'll have to give me what strength you can. But I promise I'll get you out, John."

Lindsey paused and raised her head to look him in the eyes. "Is your name really John?"

He blinked twice and a real smile spread across her kissable lips. She ducked her head to press her lips against his face. "Very nice to meet you, John Andrews."

He blinked twice. This woman offered him a way out, hope, and a chance to break free and wreak havoc on an organization that needed to crumble. She needed evidence? He'd give her everything he knew, right down to the way they snagged their victims. Hell, he'd sit with a sketch artist to describe each and every woman he remembered.

Lindsey drew back and smiled at him. "I'll be back tonight to check on you and make sure they're following my instructions on your care." Her gaze skittered down his body and she took a deep breath. "My goodness, you're beautiful." She gave his semi-hard shaft one farewell stroke before she retreated to the door. "Don't worry, John. I plan on using that cock again soon."

Lindsey grinned before ducking through the door. It clanged shut with finality, but he held on to the hope she'd engendered. She'd made small changes, but it was enough to restore his patience. He was a SEAL, and SEALs could outwait anyone. *Hell, it's only two days at most. Two days is nothing.* With his balls finally empty, Bronco settled down to sleep.

# CHAPTER FOUR

Friday morning couldn't come fast enough for Lindsey. She had to go through the motions of being the Black Widow, and that included shopping at the Forum Shoppes in Caesar's Palace and lunch with her "friends" Thursday afternoon. She had to play the part, but the overindulgent lifestyle wore thin and the edges had begun to fray.

As promised, she checked in on John and made sure the techs only gave him her new prescription of ketamine, but she retreated to her suite and went to bed early. Everything hinged on the meeting with her handler in the morning and nervous excitement ate at her. *Damn, I'm twitchier than a greyhound at the track.*

Lindsey woke before her alarm and shot out of bed to start her day. But in the shower, her *Muay Thai* instructor's voice *tsk*ed with disapproval from her memories.

"Too much mind, Ms. Lindsey. Too much mind. If you're too aware of yourself, you will show your strike before you make it." Master Chaiya's serene, weathered face nodded in her mind's eye. "Be like the wind in the grass. So ubiquitous as to go unnoticed despite its motion. They should not see you coming until it is too late"

Lindsey remembered the roundhouse kick he'd landed before she noticed. Damn, for such a small man, he'd had a hell of a lot of power. Closing her eyes, Lindsey allowed the water to wash away her tension and let her thoughts go with it.

"Very good, Ms. Lindsey. Become the façade they wish you to be. In this way, they will not see where you are going, only where you have been."

By the time she finished her shower, her Black Widow façade settled over her like a soft glove and all signs of tension had disappeared from her reflection. Lindsey raised her chin and smiled. *I got this and I'll get John clear. It's all wind in the grass from here on out.*

She dressed in one of her favorite summer dresses, a soft gold confection with spaghetti straps and a handkerchief hem. *It will complement John's eyes.* Her mind filled with a vision of them standing together as a real couple and a sense of longing filled her chest for a moment.

*Get that vision out of there before you break your cover. You don't know him beyond a cock in your hand and a body on the slab.* Lindsey took a deep breath and allowed only the good feelings of being with John to filter into her mind. The Black Widow liked feeling good and having things her way made her happy. *John makes you happy.* He did and she'd leave it at that.

She arrived at the Blue Bean a few minutes late—usual for her persona—and strode inside with her 'royal bitch' mask in place. Courtney waved from a booth near a sunny window and she nodded back before ordering her sweet and creamy coffee. She splurged on a raspberry scone and joined Court at the table.

"How was the send-off for Scouts this morning?" Lindsey settled herself after giving Courtney air-kisses.

"Good. And they won't be back until dinner time on Sunday. I get the whole weekend to play." Courtney wiggled a little in her seat, but her eyes showed none of her gaiety.

"Excellent. Can I entice you to come with me to the Club this weekend? It'll be fun." Lindsey smiled around a bite of scone.

"Not this time, sweetie. Bill and I are going to take advantage of Jeremy's absence and make it a stay-cation."

Lindsey snorted. "Ugh, why are you still with that one man? Don't you remember that line from the Robin Hood movie? *Allah wishes wondrous variety.* Where's the variety, Court?"

"Heh. I'm done with variety. I had enough of that just trying to find someone worth all the effort." Courtney rolled her eyes. "I suspect you'll get to that point soon enough, Jenna."

Lindsey raised her chin. "Not today."

"No, I suppose not." Courtney sipped her coffee. "Oh, I wanted to show you. I was at the Marie Kinney counter at the mall yesterday and they were handing out free samples of mascara. I know how much you love their cosmetics, so I grabbed one for you."

Courtney looked excited. Lindsey couldn't find a crack in her disguise at all. *Damn, she's good. That's why she's the handler and I'm the undercover cop.* Courtney grabbed her purse and pulled out a little paper gift bag in traditional Marie Kinney pink. She handed it to Lindsey and though she smiled, her eyes filled with solemnity.

"They also had lip gloss, foundation, and moisturizing cream. I got you a little sampler."

Before taking this gig, Lindsey wouldn't have known mascara from eyeliner, but Jenna Black was a woman who kept up with the Joneses and knew all the makeup and which brands were best.

"Oh, thank you so much. I was almost out of their Luscious Lash mascara." She pulled out the tube of mascara and surveyed it. The lab guys had outdone themselves in terms of disguise. She'd never know it held a syringe unless she opened it. "This is perfect. Thanks again."

"No problem, Jenna. I know you go through that stuff like water."

"And I love it, too." Lindsey winked and dropped the little pink bag into her purse. She had the nullifier, now she just needed the safe house. "So tell me about this stay-cation." She tightened her lips. "Are you going to the lake house this weekend?"

"No, it still has to be cleaned from the last time my sister was in town. You know how she parties." Courtney grimaced and shook her head. "Apparently, she'd vomited all over the carpet in the guest room and the whole house smells like stomach acid."

Lindsey's gut sank. No safe house. "Oh, that's awful. How soon can it be cleaned? I'd hate for you to miss the opportunity to get away kid-free."

Courtney laughed. "You just wanted to house-sit, didn't you?"

Lindsey bit her lip. "Guilty as charged. You have such a lovely view of Lake Las Vegas. Are you sure you can't go?"

"Bill and I are thinking of maybe renting one of the cabins up at Mt. Charleston for the weekend. I'm sure we'll come up with something. Don't worry." Courtney reached out and firmly squeezed Lindsey's hand. "But I have other good news. Remember that guy you told me about? The cute one from the same party where my sister over-indulged?"

"Yes." Lindsey stuck her tongue out for effect. "Don't tell me. He's married."

"No, silly." Courtney laughed and pulled out a card in a lavender envelope. "I got his name, number, and address for you. It's all there." She grinned. "Are you going to call him?"

"Well, aren't you just the little matchmaker." Lindsey

matched her grin and threw in a wink. "I might."

"Oh, come on, Jenna. He was cute."

"He was. But I like to keep my options open. You know, wondrous variety?"

"Yes, yes. Well, at least check him out. You might find more of value than you first thought."

Lindsey ignored the foreboding in Courtney's voice and nodded with an easy smile as she dropped the card in her purse beside the Marie Kinney bag. Both items called to her with a siren's song of temptation, but she steadfastly ignored them as she finished her coffee and scone with Courtney.

Keeping relaxed proved to be a challenge as her mind churned with concern over the safe house. Courtney promised her something when she said they'd rent, but Lindsey was running out of time. John couldn't stay under much longer. Not without endangering his health. Hell, the detox from even this amount of time would be painful.

"Well, I gotta run and take care of that cabin rental." Courtney gathered up her trash and dumped it in the nearest can before grabbing her purse. "What's your day looking like?"

"I haven't quite decided. I think I might run to the gym today before I get a manicure." Lindsey rose and hooked her purse over her shoulder, careful not to lose the bag or card. "My nails are a little ragged and I want to look my best."

"Are you going to the club tonight?" Courtney's question held a wealth of meaning.

"It depends on if I can get ahold of this guy." Lindsey patted her purse and smiled. "It might be fun to have a little company." They both laughed. "Let me know how it goes with your stay-cation."

"Will do. Laters."

Lindsey strode to her car and sat inside, chewing her lower lip. This part of the game sucked. She couldn't move forward until Courtney gave her the word, but John was running out of time and needed to be pulled out. *So come up with Plan Bravo.* If Courtney couldn't arrange a safe house, Lindsey had to find an alternative, even if it meant going dark for a while.

*So what will you do, Jarvis? Where could you go without anyone finding you?*

She backed her car out of its slot and turned onto Charleston Boulevard, heading west. She blindly drove toward Red Rock Canyon with the tourists, her mind churning with any possibility to get John out safely.

Sunlight slanted off the walls of red-striped sandstone ahead of her as she pulled into a public overlook and parked. Red Rock had always been one of the places she'd felt peaceful and safe as a kid. The ancient stone had weathered more problems than could be dreamt of in a single human lifetime, and such endurance gave her the courage to face her own challenges.

The overlook stood relatively empty in the mid-morning heat. Lindsey took a deep breath as she listened to the wind and crickets rattling in the brush. Hooking a hip on the retaining wall, she settled against the warm stone and pulled the lavender envelope out of her purse. She scanned the overlook steeling herself for whatever lay within the folded paper. Only a desert tortoise methodically picking his way among the creosote bushes kept her company.

She opened the envelope and pulled out a letter. Lindsey snorted with amusement. Only Courtney would put official information on pale lilac paper with lacy filigree along the top edge.

*Chief Petty Officer John Hector Andrews, US Navy. DOB May 22 19...* The ink smudged over the year, but she wasn't worried about his age. *Stationed in Little Creek, Virginia until June 10th. Expected in Coronado, California July 1st for a Permanent Change of Station.* Only ten days remained in June. John wouldn't be missed until a week from Monday. At least she wouldn't have the Navy breathing down her neck anytime soon.

*If he's traveling across country, he'd have a car full of stuff, probably.*

She'd have to text Courtney to have his vehicle found and impounded to return to him when he got out of this mess. *If he gets out. What the hell am I going to do with him if Court can't get a safe house?*

Her gaze drifted from the motion of a ground squirrel skittering through the brush toward the striped walls to the west. Beyond them lay dry mountains for a few miles before dropping down into the valley housing Pahrump. *Little pink houses for you and me, right?* Amusement dragged a smile across her lips before it faded into memory.

Lindsey had spent summers in Pahrump when in elementary school. Her paternal uncle and aunt had a cabin in the little town of Alpine Springs located at the pass between Vegas and Pahrump. It served as a retreat from the Mojave heat. Her uncle's cabin sat nestled in a secluded spot across Windfall creek from any neighbors. She'd only visited as a kid and since going undercover she'd had to let familial connections go. But she doubted her uncle would have disposed of the cabin.

*Plan Bravo.*

Pulling a lighter out of her purse, she lit the lacy paper on fire and watched it burn against the rough rock of the retaining wall. If Courtney couldn't get her a safe house, she'd take John to her uncle's cabin and hide out there until the coast was clear. She snorted. *Great adage, Jarvis, considering your victim is a Navy guy.*

When the paper turned to black ash, Lindsey retreated to her car and got in. She pulled out of the overlook and headed west up 160 toward Pahrump. Better to check if the cabin was occupied now than have to be surprised when she really needed it.

Her mind worked on a plan for the forty-five minute drive to Alpine Springs. By the time she turned off the highway onto the unlined road to her uncle's cabin, she'd already compiled a list of what she'd need to hole-up for a few days. She slowed down as she approached the cabin, not wanting to see anyone she knew from her previous life. This would only work as a safe house if no one knew where she'd gone.

The small A-frame building sat alone in the clearing and the robust weeds in the drive suggested no one had been there for a while. *Perfect.* She parked before the weathered front door with a small square window at eye level and got out. The temperature sat at least ten degrees cooler than Vegas here in the Spring Mountains and the warm vanilla scent of ponderosa pine filled the clearing. *Just like John.* The thought cheered her more than it should have, but she shoved it aside as she searched for the extra key. She hoped it remained hidden beneath the third loose rock in the sandstone flowerbed border just as it had her last summer there.

Relief poured through her as she grasped the cool metal. She quickly replaced the rock and returned to the door. The interior of the cabin sat in musty darkness and more of Lindsey's tension fled. She pushed open some of the drapes to let in the light. The floors had been swept and the counters washed recently. *Shit, would they come back this weekend? Think, Jarvis!* Father's Day weekend had already passed and she recalled her uncle coming to the cabin every year to celebrate.

If they'd come for Father's Day, more than likely, they wouldn't be back until Fourth of July and she had at least ten days before they returned for the holiday weekend. *That should be enough time to get him safely out and cleaned up.* John would need the detox time from the chemical cocktail LeBeau pumped into him.

Lindsey flipped on the lights, grateful for the soft glow of low wattage. John probably wouldn't like bright light. She checked the pilot light on the stove and water heater to be sure they'd have gas, and opened the kitchen taps. The water ran clear.

"Good." The house would be ready for them. If not that night, then on Saturday. *If Courtney doesn't come up with another option.*

Lindsey turned off all the lights, checked the doors and windows, and retreated to her car. Now all she had to do was wait. Her jaw tightened as she headed back to the highway. Waiting sucked. To distract herself, she ran over the list of items she'd need if they stayed at the cabin. Non-perishables, can-opener, bottled water, flashlight, blankets, men's clothing, shoes...

*Burner phone and a suit. He has to look great for the Club.*

But she just had to get him out. No one would be looking at the brand or cut in the darkness of the Club. Once in the car, it wouldn't matter. Excitement tightened her belly. They'd be out in less than thirty-six hours, and John would be safe.

# CHAPTER FIVE

Lindsey took a deep breath as she waited for the valet. Her mind rechecked her inventory to make sure she hadn't forgotten anything. She had her own casual clothes in addition to what she'd purchased the day before. Jenna Black would go missing that evening, right along with Chief Petty Officer JH Andrews.

Squaring her shoulders, Lindsey pulled up to the valet and smiled at the young man who waited for her to get out. *Show time.*

"Good afternoon, Ms. Black. Are you leaving your car with us today?"

"Hello, Pedro. I am. I need it to be taken care of tonight. I have a date." She gave him a smug smile.

"Oh-ho, this I've got to see. The infamously single Ms. Black with a man? You've dashed my hopes." He theatrically threw a hand over his heart and staggered back a step.

Lindsey laughed. She'd miss the young man. "Yes, I'm sure. Please be sure it is safe and secure. I don't want my plans messed up."

"Of course, Ms. Black. You can count on me." His smile widened as she slipped him a fifty dollar bill.

"You're always so good to me."

"I know you want to go to college and it costs. Education is very important, Pedro."

"I know, I know. I remember. I won't let you down, Ms. Black."

"Excellent. I'll see you tonight with my date." Lindsey waved as she pulled the suit bag out of the passenger door and headed for the hotel.

Everything was in order. Courtney had called to say still no safe house, but Lindsey had figured it would be the case. She'd replied she hoped they still had a nice time and she had a date with the guy in the card.

"He said yes? That's great. When?"

"Tonight. I'll call you when I get back."

"You're sure you're okay with not house-sitting?"

"Yes, I'll be fine. You know you're ruining my weekend plans, don't you?"

Courtney had snorted. "Yeah, right. I know you. You always land on your feet, Jenna."

She couldn't argue with that. They'd signed off and Lindsey had put her all her attention into Plan Bravo. She allowed a confident smile to crease her lips as she hugged her purse to her side. The Luscious Lash syringe case and the burner phone sat snug in the zippered pockets. She'd activated the phone that morning, but hadn't turned it on since. No point in using it until necessary.

When she arrived in her suite, she hung John's suit and unzipped the bag. It wouldn't fool anyone on close inspection, but in a Club with hundreds of people jostling in strobe lights, he'd look like a decent date for Mistress Black. She'd dated a few others in her term undercover just to give legitimacy to such activities, but she'd never run with a man before.

*Here's hoping I make a decent kidnapper.*

She snorted as she sat at her little laptop and typed out a request for her toy to be delivered to her suite that evening. While not common to have a private audience with purchased products, it was allowed upon occasion. *This is a great occasion.* Lindsey hit enter and headed for the shower. Anything to calm the excitement building as the time approached. She had to be cool or she'd give away the whole game. *And I'm not losing this one.*

**\*\*\*\***

Lindsey's cell rattled out the *Ride of the Valkyries* as she put the finishing touches on her makeup. She really did appreciate Courtney's little gift and gave herself a false smile as she picked up her phone.

"Hello?"

"Hey, Jenna. I just wanted to see how you're doing. Date night tonight, right?" Courtney's voice sounded excited, but Lindsey suspected that hid the anxiousness.

*Or maybe it's my anxiousness I'm reading into it.*

"Yes, tonight is the night. I got the confirmation he'd be here in… Ooo, five minutes." She checked her hair and lip gloss in the mirror then left the bathroom for the main suite.

"Are you staying in or going out?"

"I think we'll have drinks here, then head to the club. Why?"

"I just want to make sure you're safe. Men can be a handful, you know. Especially this guy. He's so big." Courtney hinted at John's strength and training.

Lindsey forced a laugh. "I'm sure we'll be okay, but I'll be careful. This Club takes a dim view on physical abuse and I'll be surrounded by people. Don't worry, Court. I'll be fine."

"All right. I just want you to know I'm here for you and you can call me any time."

"Thanks, Court. He's meeting me at the hotel, but left his car where he's staying. I'm sure it'll be great. He'll at least need to be nice to me to get a ride back."

"Did he tell you his hotel?"

"No, but I can probably weasel it out of him."

Lindsey heard keys tapping in the background. Courtney already started the search for John's car. "Good. Just be safe and have fun tonight, 'kay?"

"Will do. Say hi to Bill for me and you kids have fun, too."

"We will. Bye."

"Bye."

A knock at her suite door made Lindsey snap her phone shut and smooth down her dress. *It's the moment of truth.* She strode to the door and pulled it open, trying not to show her disgust at the vision of John Andrews strapped to a board on a dolly. She covered it with a smile she could only hope appeared pleased.

"Excellent, wheel him over to the bed."

The orderlies nodded as they delivered her package and she ignored the urge to pull out her weapon and shoot them both. Instead, she left the door open, an implicit request to leave. They hauled him up on the bed and rolled the dolly out into the living space.

"If I want to keep him longer than my arranged time, I'll send in a new request. I'll get a confirmation email, isn't that so?"

"You will."

Resisting the urge to untie him before they'd gone, Lindsey followed them out of the bedroom and picked up her purse. She pulled out two twenties and extended it to the taller orderly.

"Thank you, ma'am. Much appreciated."

"No, thank you."

"We'll be back in two hours to re-administer his meds or take him back to the holding cells."

"Thank you. I'll be ready."

The orderly nodded and the two men left, closing the

door behind them. Lindsey turned the security lock and engaged the security bar then took a deep breath. If she had any say in the matter, neither she nor John would be here when they returned.

Lindsey grabbed a glass in her kitchenette and filled it with water to calm her nerves. She'd swept the room for bugs earlier, but her whole mission depended upon her appearing completely at ease. *Even if they can't see or hear me.* She refused to admit her nervousness came from the man lying on the bed in the other room.

She gulped down the last of her water and headed for the room. He needed to be untied and dressed. She chuckled and shook her head. *This isn't going to be like dressing a baby doll.* None of her dolls had ever been fully articulated, much less anatomically correct.

The orderlies had laid him on the bed on his back, his hands and ankles bound. Growling, she darted to her purse. She might only have a small decorative pocketknife, but zipties still broke before steel. Who knew a TV show would come in so handy? *Rule number nine: Always carry a knife.*

"Hang on, John. I'll have them off soon." She snapped the ties at his ankles with one swipe of the little blade, but the bonds on his wrists took some sawing. Fury brewed with each cut through the plastic. "We'll get you out of here and bring the sick bastards down."

The zipties fell away and she tossed the knife back into her purse before settling down beside him. Deep welts marked the skin at his wrists. He stared straight up at the ceiling and she angled his head toward her so she could meet his gaze as she rubbed his hands.

"Sit tight. Let me get the nullifier into you so it can work its magic before I get your circulation going again." Lindsey rose and dug through her purse, retrieving the syringe disguised as the mascara tube. "Ready?"

John blinked twice. *Yes.*

"You're stronger than you think and this will work fast." Faster than two hours at least. *That's all I need.*

She swallowed against revulsion as she readied the needle. She could face down a jacked-up junkie with a loaded weapon, but one little needle entering skin made her want to run screaming for the hills. *Just push it in and be done, Jarvis.*

Lindsey pressed the plunger to let out the air and inserted the needle into his vein. She kept her mind on the feel of his warm skin in her hands to push off the threatening nausea. *Focus.* At last the plunger hit bottom and she pulled the syringe out.

"There. That should do it." She glanced at his eyes. "At least get it started." She deposited the used syringe back into her purse. "Let me get you a towel." She selected one of the fluffy burgundy towels from her bath and returned to the bedroom. "This will be like a swanky massage, right?" She gave him a half smile as she laid the towel over his lap and tucked it around his hips. When done, she sat down beside him, certain to keep in his line of sight.

"I guess we have a little time to get to know each other."

She paused, resisting the urge to run her hands over the taut muscles of his legs. She'd learned the softness of his hair and ached to touch it again. *You get no liberties now, Jarvis.* "So I did some checking and I found out you're in the Navy headed to Coronado Naval Base on a Permanent Change of Station. Is that right?"

Lindsey met his gaze and he blinked twice. "I know the Naval SpecOps trains there." She scanned his body. "And no tattoos, which is unusual. Most military guys get tats, but not you."

The scars stood out against his tanned skin, but no ink. "Unless you've removed them, which leaves bad scars and hurts like hell, so I'm told. Did you once have a tat, John?"

He blinked once and she nodded. "Me, either. Given my job, I don't want too many indentifying marks."

She leaned forward and glanced down at her feet, suddenly nervous. *What are you, a teenager on a first date? You've had sexual intimacies with this man. You aren't strangers.*

Lindsey scooted back on the bed closer to John so he could see her better. "Do you want me to prop you up on pillows so you have a better view of the room?"

John blinked twice and she smiled. "Yeah, I figured you'd prefer to be able to see all escape routes, even if you can't use them." She crawled behind him and looped her hands under his arms then pulled back toward the headboard.

"Holy moly, you're heavy." She succeeded in moving him only inches. *Damn, remind me not to go out for SpecOps in the military any time soon.* "I'll pile pillows behind you and prop you up. It might be just as well. I'll have to dress you and it'll be easier if your legs are near the floor."

She slid out from behind him and rested on the bed. "Damn, you smell good. At least they finally gave you a bath." He didn't say anything and she wished an end to the one-sided conversation. "I feel like I'm talking to myself, you know?"

John blinked two times and moaned. Lindsey gasped. "I heard you. This is a good sign the nullifier is working." John's lids fluttered with agreement.

"So I'm sure you're wondering at my plan." She rolled over so they lay nose to nose. He blinked twice. "I figure you're going to be unsteady on your feet and slurring words. The perfect cover has us as a drunken couple leaving the Man Cave Club downstairs. My handler couldn't get a safe house set up in time, but you can't stay here longer. The ketamine will shut down your heart and other organs. We weren't given a choice so I found my own safe house. Once we're out of the club we'll head straight there. Copy?"

John blinked twice again.

"I promise I'll get you out and keep you safe until you come down off the ketamine. Then we can bring you in." She ignored the pang at how little time she'd have to spend with him alone. *This is a job, Jarvis. You don't even know this man very well.*

It didn't stop her desire to know him better. Unfortunately, he couldn't answer any complex questions. Yes and no was all they had at the moment. Lindsey studied his golden-brown eyes full of intelligence below the thick brows. She wondered what his face would look like with full animation. Did he have dimples in his cheeks? Crow's feet at the edges of his eyes? She still didn't know how old he was, but he didn't look too much older than her.

John groaned and his brows contracted a little.

"Sorry, am I hurting you?"

John blinked once and she sighed. "I wish I could talk to you in more than just yes or no questions." His eyes closed twice to show his agreement. "Tell, you what, let's get you dressed so you're ready to go when the ketamine wears off."

Lindsey didn't wait for his agreement as she slid off the bed and headed for the luxurious walk-in closet. She opened the suit bag and pulled out the dark pinstriped jacket and pants. She hoped she'd estimated his size right. She carried it out to show him and tried to ignore how beautiful he looked lying there on the bed. *Focus, Jarvis.*

"So what do you think? It's a size forty jacket to fit those shoulders of yours and size thirty-thirty-two pants. Did I get them right?"

She thought she read surprise in his eyes before he closed them twice. Pleasure bloomed in her chest at her good guesses and she smiled.

"I didn't know your size of shirt, so I made sure it had

a seventeen inch neck and short sleeves. I didn't have a lot of time to look." She held up a packaged button-down shirt. "Think it will fit?"

John's brows lowered a little and he blinked twice.

Lindsey nodded. "Good. Let's try it, shall we?"

She laid the suit over the nearest chair and opened the shirt package before she climbed onto the bed. He watched her, the corner of his mouth twitching.

"Are you smiling at me, John?"

His eyes closed twice more and she answered with a grin. "When I was a little girl, I didn't have a baby doll, but my mother insisted I had to learn to play with those vegetable patch kids. She bought me one and I thought it was the ugliest thing out there." Lindsey pulled the cardboard insert out of the shirt and shook out the cloth. "I thought cream would look great against your tanned skin."

John grunted and she took it as amusement.

"Anyway, undressing and dressing that thing was a pain in the ass. It had thick, chubby arms and legs, and the clothes would stick to the fabric of the doll. I think I gave up after the second outfit."

She reached for his arm and gathered the heavy limb, enjoying the scent of his skin and the rough texture of his palm. She rubbed the calluses with her thumbs, noting the locations of them. The calluses spoke of experience and understanding of weapons. Something about them sent excitement shooting to her groin. *Damn, military men are sexy.*

"You have beautiful hands, John." She turned his arm over to look at the veins and muscles beneath the dark hair of his forearm. "I love the strength in them. They show your experience without being ostentatious. You don't have to scream about your knowledge. Your body shows your capabilities." She raised her gaze to his. "It's beautiful."

\*\*\*\*

John didn't think he'd ever had a woman tell him she found him beautiful. In his line of work, beauty wasn't an attribute they strove for. But something about the way Lindsey held and caressed his hand made him grateful she saw him as beautiful. He wanted to tell her she held as much beauty and sensual grace as she attributed to him, but his voice still refused to work.

Lindsey seemed to come back to herself and gave him an apologetic smile. "Sorry, I got a little carried away there. Dressing you shouldn't be as hard as the doll. At least the cloth won't snag on your skin."

She fit the open shirt sleeve over his left hand and dragged it up to his bicep in gentle tugs. She shifted behind him to lift up his shoulders and her cherry-blossom fragrance washed over him. He closed his eyes and reveled in it. *God, she smells so good.* The scent-memory would stay with him forever.

"Heh, even your chest and shoulders are heavy." Lindsey pushed him up and propped him on her chest. He enjoyed the soft swells of her breasts against his bare back. *Too bad she's still wearing her dress.* He hadn't had the pleasure of skin on skin with her. *Dammit.*

She tugged the shirt around his shoulders then paused, giving a short laugh. "This would be so much easier if you could help me. Okay, up you go." She shoved him into a sitting position, grunting with her efforts. The world spun as his head sagged and her arms wrapped around him to keep him upright. *Well, kinda upright.* He swayed and tilted, and his own frustration echoed the low growl rumbling in her chest against his back.

"This is so wrong, it's funny." She laid her head on his shoulder and took a few breaths. "Okay, I think I have to roll you onto your belly, lift your other arm to get it in the sleeve, then roll you back. God help me when I have to get the jacket on you. Ready?"

What could he say? She sat behind him and he couldn't turn his head.

"All right. Here we go."

She scooted out from behind him and gently laid him on his back. "Are we good?"

He blinked twice and mentally grinned at her.

"Good." She nodded. "Onto your stomach, now. I'll try to make sure you can breathe."

She straightened out his limbs then pushed him over onto his belly, shifting the towel to drape over his ass. When his nose flattened against the bed, she gently turned his head to the side. His view filled with pillow and wall, but he heard Lindsey get off the bed and rustle around in the room.

"I know you can't see me, but I think I should do the jacket, too. I don't think I have the strength to keep rolling you over."

Not to mention he didn't enjoy smelling the bedding. He tried to tell her he thought her idea a good one, but it came out as a muffled moan.

"Okay, I'll try to make it quick."

Cool fabric rested on his thighs as she returned to the bed, the mattress dipping with her weight. She tugged the shirt over his shoulders then slid her hands down his arm to grasp his wrist. Every motion seemed like a sensuous dance of texture, and he closed his eyes to savor the feeling of her soft skin. She lifted his free arm and fed it through the arm hole, gently straightening it and laying it beside his body.

"I should have done this to begin with." Her mutter made him laugh inwardly.

His thighs cooled as she lifted the suit jacket and worked one arm then the other into it. When she had it settled across his shoulders, she paused and her hands smoothed the fabric down his back. *What is she doing?* When her hands continued off the coat and onto his towel-covered ass, he stopped caring why. The heat of her palms through the cloth seared him and he sighed, his cock hardening with her touch.

"I love your ass. I know it's not professional to tell you that or to touch you, but I want you to know I appreciate your body. Too weird?"

John took a deep breath. "Uh-uh."

Okay, not the most eloquent, but a step in the right direction. The nullifier had kicked in.

Lindsey reached around him and pulled him over onto his back, tugging out the towel to re-cover his lap. Her gaze searched his with hopeful intensity. "So it's not too weird that I find you beautiful?"

"Uh-uh."

The smile cascading across her face blinded him with its glorious beauty. He wanted to make her smile like that more. *Yeah, good luck with that, Andrews. She's an undercover cop in Vegas and you're a SEAL headed for Coronado.* It didn't stop him from wanting to find out more about her. He desired it more than he'd wished for anything since joining the SEALs. More than he wanted the plum assignment of Team 9, Bravo Squad under Lieutenant Commander Whittleton.

Lindsey studied him a short time before she set down the towel and straightened his clothes around his body. "It's a shame to cover this up." She slid her hand over his furred chest and his nipples peaked in anticipation of her caress. "Oh, God, I sound like my Black Widow persona." Her mouth curled into a frown as she reached for the buttons on the shirt.

"Uh-uh!"

Lindsey paused and raised her eyebrows. "You don't want me to button the shirt?"

John blinked once. He wanted more touches, more closeness with her. He didn't know how much time they had. Once they left the hotel, any intimacy would be over.

Lindsey tipped her head, biting her bottom lip. "Would

you, um…" A warm blush stained her cheeks. "Would you like to have sex, John?"

Bronco moaned, closing his eyes with *hell yes* ringing in his head. "Uh-huh." His cock thickened and flexed in agreement.

Lindsey gave a breathy laugh and John opened his eyes just as one hand peeled away the towel and the other closed around his shaft. God, her touch flooded his awareness with pleasure, and she hadn't even stroked him yet. He moaned his appreciation and tried to tighten his hands into fists. To his delighted surprise, his fingers moved a little.

"I see your hands are moving. That's good." Lindsey slid down his body and released his cock. When he moaned in protest, she stroked his thighs, each gentle touch stealing some of his concentration. "Don't worry, John. I just think we should get your pants started before we do anything. I want to be sure you're ready to go."

"Huh?"

"You'll have to go commando. I hope you're okay with that." The sultry, heavy-lidded look she gave him said she didn't care if he shared her opinion or not. "Besides, how will I enjoy your cock if it's covered in cotton?"

He didn't care how she enjoyed it, just that she did.

She hopped off the bed, the skirt of her little black dress swaying with sensual invitation, and pulled the suit pants off their hanger. When she turned back to him, the smile curling her lips sent erotic excitement shooting straight to his balls. She looked ready to torture him with pleasure.

Lindsey knelt where his feet hung off the bed and he lost sight of her. But her hands caressed one ankle and tingles ran to his groin. Damn, even invisible, this woman excited him.

"Let's get these pants on up to your thighs at least. Then I'll take my time with you. Does that sound good, John?"

*Do they race horses at the Kentucky Derby?* "Uh-huh."

She chuckled and it sent his brain into a spiral. So sexy. *They should use her in interrogation. Men would spill their secrets just to hear her laugh.*

She worked the pants over both feet and pulled them up his legs, taking her time stroking and caressing each muscle group. John's cock flexed and jerked with desperation, the need for her touch almost painful. He groaned.

"What, John?" She tugged the pants up nearly to his hips as she lifted one leg then the other. "Do you need something?"

The diabolical woman slid her hands around his bare hips and worked her fingers into the hairs on his groin. Holy shit, each subtle motion set off a conflagration of sensation, tightening his balls and the muscles of his belly.

"Mmm, I like that. Each one of your abdominals flexes when I touch you." She did it again and his gut rippled. "Oh, yeah, so nice."

Nice didn't even begin to cover it.

"As much as I'd like to dwell on your lovely physique, my pussy is wet and achy, and I haven't had a cock in it for a long time. Do you think I could borrow yours?"

"Uh-huh!" The woman had a mouth like a sailor and he loved it. She had elegance and grace, yet she was hot and dirty and so damn sexy. *I need her when we're out of this op.*

He'd never met a woman with such charisma and command. Yet, he sensed softness mixed in, a feminine quality to balance out the toughness. *She's perfect.* He just had to figure out how to make her his when they found the clear water.

# CHAPTER SIX

Lindsey thanked her lucky stars John agreed to her request. She'd given up on being professional and just needed to fuck this man. His sexy body had teased her for days and she'd always had an audience, so using his cock to pleasure her pussy had been out of the question. But they finally had some time alone and he seemed to want sex as badly as she did.

*Thank God.*

"Oh, good. Because your cock is just begging for a taste. Oooh, and my pussy wants it so much, John."

He groaned and closed his eyes briefly. His hands tightened on the covers and he moved his hips a little.

*Yes, it's working.*

"Let me get a condom and then I'm going to feast on you."

A tortured groan echoed behind her as she strode to her purse. She didn't think they had time for more than one orgasm, but she'd take what she could get. *It might be my only chance to enjoy him.* She ignored the sense of loss squeezing her chest as she returned to the bed.

She held up the condom packet and smiled. "Are you ready for me, John?"

"Yeaaaaahhhh." The word was slurred, but he'd gained use of his tongue again.

*Too bad he can't use it on me.* She shoved her inner harlot to the back of her mind. *Later.*

"Very good. Let me just make sure your dick is as hard as I need it."

Lindsey knelt between his legs and stoked his thighs up to his groin, nuzzling his balls with her nose. "Oooh, John, you smell so good. Let me see how you taste today."

She grasped his shaft and pulled it to her lips, extending her tongue to lick the head. The muscles in her grip jerked as she slid her tongue over edge of the glans and engulfed the taut head with her mouth. John whimpered and Lindsey grinned around his shaft.

His musky, salty taste hit her tongue and she damn near swooned. She could lick him for hours, but her pussy reminded her it had been neglected for far too long. She inhaled his warm vanilla scent and stroked his shaft with the flat of her tongue. His hips rose in minute jerks as he regained control and she encouraged him by tightening her lips around his cock.

"Oh, John, that's it. Move for me." Lindsey fondled his balls with the tips of her fingers and he moaned. The hard flesh in her mouth thickened and jerked with his arousal, and she couldn't wait any longer.

"I need you, John. I need to ride you like a bucking bronco."

He whimpered again and his lips pulled back from his teeth a little. Damn, he'd be sexy when he smiled. She wished she could see that when he came. *Soon.*

"Are you ready for me, my bronco? This cowgirl wants to ride hard."

"Yeeaahhh...fffuck...mmmee...hard."

Lindsey hummed with delight as she ripped open the condom packet. "Oh, he uses words at last. Your wish is my command, John."

She fit the latex over his rigid shaft and crawled onto his lap. She lifted her handkerchief hem out of the way and reached between his legs to position his cock at her nether lips. "Are you ready for me, bronco mine?"

"Rogerr…that."

"Oh, yeeeaaaahhh." Lindsey loved the military response as she sank down on his hard cock. "Oh, God, you're so thick." Pleasure spread from her groin up her back and she shivered with delirious joy.

"Rrride mme…cowgirl." His hips twitched and his hands gripped the comforter as her inner muscles squeezed his flesh

Lindsey rocked her hips, bracing her weight on his chest, and she stared down at his golden brown eyes. They glowed with inner fire and it set her arousal ablaze. He might not be able to speak, but his expression told her he wanted this. Something about turning a man on warmed her more than just getting pleasure. She wanted to share the ecstasy with her partner, not just take it from him.

"Come on, bronco mine, let me ride you. Let me drive you hard." She squeezed his cock as she bent forward to suck on a nipple.

John groaned and gently thrust into her. She wished they could go harder, but he still had only minimal control of his body. *Then I'll just have to ride him harder myself.* She pushed her hips off his lap and slammed them back down. They both grunted with the impact, but pleasure shot through her to explode out of the crown of her head. John growled in the back of his throat and his eyes narrowed as he grimaced with effort.

"Oh, you like that, do you, my bronco?" She rose and dropped hard again, and he repeated his growl. "Oh, yeah, you do. Let me hear your joy."

She rocked on him, grinding her clit against his stiff shaft and her arousal built to a screaming pitch. Her orgasm ignited, simmering in her pussy as she slammed down on him again.

"Oh, God, John, I'm going to come. Come with me, bronco. Come hard!"

The pleasure rocketed up her spine and threw her into the starry black of orgasm. She squealed her ecstasy out as John matched her with a groan, his eyes squeezed shut. Lindsey tried to enjoy the look of his hard body taut in the throes of passion, but her orgasm tore away her sight and sent her spinning among the stars.

"Sssoo…good, Lindsey."

The sound of his careful voice brought her back to herself and she met his gaze. The expression on his face warmed her thundering heart. He looked content, satisfied, all the good adjectives she'd ever learned in school. She tightened her internal muscles around him and bent down to kiss him, suddenly realizing she hadn't ever done so.

His lips moved under hers and opened for her tongue. Hot vanilla spice filled her mouth as his tongue slid past hers and her pussy spasmed with erotic pleasure. Damn, she'd already come hard, but the slick texture set her arousal on fire.

Unfortunately, her phone pinged with her alarm for ten P.M. The club would be rocking and they could get out without being noticed now. It reminded her she actually had a job to do beyond enjoying the man between her legs.

Lindsey sat up and gave him an apologetic smile. "Sorry, John. It's time to go. You ready to get out of this prison?"

His gaze slid over her face, down to her taut nipples pressing against the bodice of her dress, and back to her eyes. "Wish…could…savor. But…rready."

"Me, too, John." She rose off his cock and headed for the bathroom.

"Lindsey?"

She paused at the door to the bath. "Yes?"

"Liked it…when you…called me…Bronco."

"Yeah? It suits you." She grinned at him then hurried to clean up. Her nerves still sang with the aftermath of her orgasm, but it was time to work and she had to be ready.

When she returned to the bedroom, she used a warm wash cloth to clean his softening cock and smiled at his low, rumbling growl of pleasure. She made sure to remove the condom and stroke away his cum before tossing the condom and rag in a plastic bag. *Show time.*

"Let's get you dressed all the way and we'll be out the door."

"Roger that."

"It sounds like you're getting your voice back."

"Little."

"That's not how I'd describe it." She winked.

"Heh."

Lindsey laughed and worked his dress pants up to his hips, deftly tucking his damp cock and balls inside. John grunted with her touches, but didn't protest. She buttoned his shirt and tucked only half of it into the pants before she secured the button.

"Give me a moment. I think I have a belt for you as well as a tie."

"Tie?"

"Yeah, you need to look ready for the Club, even if you've had sex before you got there." Lindsey winked again as she searched the suit bag for the articles she'd bought. The shiny, mustard yellow tie matched his eyes and she laid it over his chest while she worked on his pants. "I think I found the right sized belt. Your hips are trimmer than I remembered. Don't worry, you won't have to wear it very long."

"Already…want…me undressssssed…again?" Humor laced his slurred words.

Lindsey laughed. "Hell yeah, but I meant we can have you in sweats when we get to where we're going." She tucked in the rest of the shirt as she buckled the belt then added the tie around his neck. "There. You're a pretty sharp dressed man."

John grunted. "No beard."

"Heh, smart guy." She shook her head at his smile. "Okay, let me get your shoes on and dispose of my phone. Then we'll be ready."

He dipped his chin in a small nod and she finished dressing him. *Jeez, even his feet are sexy.* Once she had the shoes tied, she took her phone into the bath and slammed it against the marble tub. The expensive screen shattered, a spider-web of cracks radiating across the face. She removed the battery on the back and the SD card buried under it, and shoved them in her purse. She dropped the phone in the wastebasket. *Good luck finding us now.*

"Almost there." She strode through the room and deposited her purse and shoes near the door. She scanned the suite for anything that could be traced back to her once she'd gone and nodded with satisfaction. All they had to do was get out into the hallway.

Straightening her dress, she reached the bed and studied John's still form. He'd closed his eyes and looked just like an exhausted businessman collapsed on the bed. Guilt and sorrow stole some of her contentment at the bags under his eyes, but they'd needed to wait for the nullifier to work enough for him to move.

"John?"

He opened his eyes and all exhaustion left his face, replaced by a determined intensity. He might lie prone, but every inch of him screamed warrior. Wide awake and aware, he scanned her body and she hoped she measured up to whatever standard he held.

"Time to go. If I help you up, can you stay upright?"

"Don't know."

"Let's try it." She stood between his knees and reached for his arms, wrapping her hands around his wrists. Lindsey leaned back, using her knees to give her leverage to pull him upright.

The process took longer than she liked, but her strength finally overcame his inertia and he leaned forward onto her chest.

"Nice…breasts…Soft."

Lindsey laughed. "And real, too. Now, can you sit up on your own?"

"No, don't…think so."

When she stepped back, he flopped forward with her and she grunted with impact. "No, I guess not yet. How the heck am I gonna get you to the door?"

She didn't think she could do a fireman's carry with him. *He's too big and heavy for that.* And he didn't have the strength or control for staggering beside her yet. She could drag him, but she'd never get him to his feet at the door.

Lindsey glanced down at his lovely golden eyes and swore he raised a curious eyebrow at her. How else could she move him? *Too bad I don't have a luggage cart. Luggage…lugging…*

"Okay, this is going to be weird." Lindsey turned her back to John and knelt on the floor. "I'm going to wear you to the door."

"Mmmpf?" His question puffed into the hair at her nape.

"Yeah, like a cloak." She draped his arms over her shoulders. "You ready?"

"Uhhhh."

"Come on, sailor. Time to take a ride."

"Liked…the…earlier one…better."

Lindsey huffed a laugh as she settled his chest against her back. "Me too, but this isn't going to be like that." She groaned as she leaned forward on her hands and knees. "This is going to be more like the first time I touched you. Professional. Kinda."

"Would…have…given permission…then, too."

She ignored the pleasure slipping through her body with his words. Damn, she'd missed an opportunity there. But her superiors would see the video and she couldn't afford to be fired for fucking on the job.

When his weight settled onto her back, she grunted and her knees protested, but none of her joints buckled. *Score one for me.* Despite the small victory, carrying John, even the few feet to the door of the room proved difficult. Lifting each limb became an exercise in stable placement. If she didn't get the balance right, she'd end up flat on the floor with him holding her down.

Lindsey paused at the bedroom door and leaned against the jamb, catching her breath. *Holy shit, how the hell am I going to make it across the whole suite?*

"Man, you're heavy, Bronco. Let me just catch my breath."

"Take…your…time. Getting…stronger."

"Good."

Crawling to the door took every bit of strength she had and her slinky dress didn't make the best man-hauling clothes. John gathered control with every passing minute and she had to get them out of here before the orderlies came back to administer another dose of the drug. The sense of urgency gave her the extra endurance to make it to the entryway.

When she reached the doorjamb, she thanked her lucky stars she hadn't worn stockings. John turned his head to look over her right shoulder and hope sparked. If he could move that much, maybe he could stand on his own.

"Okay. Are you ready to stand now?"

"Ready…as I'll…ever be."

Lindsey shifted closer to the wall and he raised his right arm, grasping the doorframe. He pulled and his muscles bunched, but he didn't move.

"Here, wait a second." She took a deep breath. "Let me kneel up and your legs can take your weight slowly.

Okay?"

"Sounds…like a…plan."

"Ready?" Lindsey gathered her strength to push upright.

"Yeah."

Several moments of sweating and straining passed as she tried to get her shoulders up without dumping John unceremoniously onto the floor. Lindsey used the wall to brace herself and swung the other arm behind her to hold his sliding body.

"Got it?"

"Yeah. The wall is helping." She glanced over her shoulder and found him leaning against the jamb on his knees. But he remained upright.

"Think you can stand?"

"I have to, don't I?"

"Pretty much. I don't think I can haul 200 pounds of Chief Petty Officer out of here. At least not and make it look like we're supposed to be wandering around." Lindsey clambered to her feet and put on her shoes.

"How *were* you planning on getting out of here?"

"We're going to go down through the club and you're going to be my drunk boyfriend/date." She brushed off her knees and straightened her dress. "Does my hair look disheveled enough to have had drunk sex in a back room?"

John's gaze made a leisurely climb from her ankles to her head and a predatory expression settled over his features. *How can he still be horny after what we just did?* A smug smile curled his lips and he nodded.

"You do look like you've had sex recently." He inhaled and his smile widened. "You smell like it, too."

"I do?" Sheesh, so much for professionalism. "Then I'll definitely fit the part. Come on. We gotta get out of here before the drug pushers come back."

Lindsey shoved her shoulder under John's armpit and wrapped an arm around his waist. "Ready?"

"I don't have a choice, do I?"

"Get out of the hotel and the Man Cave Club, and you'll have all the choices you want."

"Then let's do this. Are there cameras in the halls?"

"Yes. Keep your head down and get your drunk on."

"Roger that."

Lindsey loved hearing those words. Something about the military remark turned her on more than flowers or jewelry. He trusted her and depended on her to get him out. His respect was a heady brew infusing her body with extra strength.

Lindsey opened the door and glanced both directions down the hallway outside. The rich brown carpet remained empty. She nodded and they staggered out the door. John took a deep breath, his hard ribs expanding against her side, and hummed.

"Are you okay?" Lindsey whispered as they meandered toward the elevators.

"Damn, baby, you're schmexy." His slurred words sounded so authentic she glanced up at him. He winked and planted a sloppy kiss on her forehead. "Where'ya takin' me now, huh?"

She giggled, hoping it sounded real. "Back to the Club where you can't get into trouble." They almost collided with the elevator doors and she twittered as she pressed the button. "Oops, sorry."

John's arm tightened around her shoulders as he swayed a little and he pressed his forehead against hers. "Cameras in the elevator, too?"

Lindsey nodded. "In all the public places."

"Copy that."

The elevator dinged and the doors slid open. Lindsey breathed a sigh of relief to find the car empty as they shuffled aboard. John let her choose the club floor then crowded her against the wall, blocking the camera with his broad back. From behind it would look like he made out with her. *Too bad it's just pretend.* Something about this man made her want more than just the mission's façade. *Maybe when it's all over I can date him for real.*

The idea lodged in her heart and planted roots. She tried not to give it much energy, but yearning and excitement zinged through her and made her heart pound. *What the hell am I thinking?* She almost shook her head, but John chose that moment to kiss her neck and she dragged her focus back to the present.

*Fantasies can wait...and he'll star in all of them from now on.*

The elevator bumped gently to a stop and John staggered back, dragging Lindsey with him as the doors hissed open. A solid wall of sound and heat flooded over them and Lindsey resisted clapping her hands over her ears. She'd forgotten how loud the club became after midnight.

"Fuck yeah, let's dance, baby!" John grabbed her in a stumbling waltz pose and thrust her out into the melee of churning bodies on the floor.

She dropped her head, pretending to watch her feet as John propelled her into the crowd. Gyrating bodies jostled them and they made slow progress toward the exit. Lindsey nearly lost her balance and dragged them both down beneath the stomping feet, but John lurched against her weight. He let out a raucous laugh at a few folks' grumbling complaints as they shoved their way through the press of undulating flesh.

Lindsey hoped the darkness and flashing lights would disguise their faces from the cameras perched in every corner of the club. Madame LeBeau would recognize her and her sailor immediately. She scanned the little alcove normally hosting the madam, but her gaze snagged on two hatchet-faced men plowing through the crowd. *Bouncers.* Gut-churning anxiety ate at her and stiffened some of her limbs. John shot a glance at her before he stopped and dragged her against his chest.

"Oh, come on, baby. Don't be like that. You know you want me." He reached around and grabbed her ass, turning her until her back faced the edge of the dance floor near the seating area.

Two bouncers shoved past behind her, one of them clipping her hip in his passage. The pain from his pinch made her jump, but she swallowed the indignant squawk. They just had to get out to the safe house and none of this would matter.

*And I'll lose John.*

The thought hollowed out her heart, but she firmly reminded herself he'd never really been hers. *Just finish the mission and get clear.* Easier said than done.

# CHAPTER SEVEN

John felt Lindsey jump as the bouncers walked by and stiffened his arms to keep from swinging at the bastards. The jackasses took advantage of the press to fondle the women they passed. He'd love to kick each over-muscled butt out the back door, but getting out undetected trumped retribution. *Ain't that always the case?*

Frankly, John was surprised the bouncers got away with it considering what kind of racket Madame LeBeau had going on. He doubted she'd take kindly to men having the upper hand, even in her club. John blearily steered Lindsey around the dance floor, trying not to jostle the other revelers, but the drugs kept him unsteady. It worked fine for the role of drunk boyfriend he played, but it hampered his ability to escape the club efficiently.

"Ms. Black, I see you've gotten a new boy toy to play with."

John released Lindsey as they swung around to face an elegantly dressed woman in crimson seated at the bar. The other woman scanned John from head to toe with lascivious interest and he let his features go slack with exaggerated drunkenness. Something about her perusal soured his stomach.

"Yes, I found him here at the Club. I'm looking forward to seeing what all he can do." Lindsey's shoulders straightened and she ran a hand possessively over John's chest. She wrapped her fist around his tie and tugged on him until he looked her in the eyes. "And you're going to do everything I ask you, aren't you, Mr. Smith?"

John swayed as he nodded dumbly. "Uh-huh. Yeah."

"Good boy." Lindsey turned her gaze back to the woman in red. "Where's your toy, Lady Katy?"

The other woman shrugged with a negligent toss of her head. "Oh, it expired recently. I'm waiting for a new replacement." Her gaze fixed on John and she licked her lips, her eyes full of avarice. "Do let me know how this one works out for you. I might want to take him for a spin if there's anything left when you're done."

Lindsey's laugh chilled John to the bone. "You know I don't leave leftovers. I use every. Last. Drop." She punctuated each word with her hand groping some part of his body until she gently squeezed his balls. He groaned as she gave her hand a vicious twist and bent over to hide her lack of real purchase. *Thank God she didn't really rip them off.*

Lady Katy squealed with delight. "Oh, he's marvelously responsive. I miss that about the toys, but one can't be too careful." She waved a hand in John's direction. "Where are you taking him?"

Strobe lights flashed as their immediate silence stretched beneath the thumping music of the Club. Lindsey kept her gaze on John as if considering the next step in a diabolical plan. Her smile came slow and sultry but cold, and John shivered despite himself.

"I want to go see the fountains and be kissed under the lights before taking him to bed."

"Aww, how romantic. I never knew you had it in you, Ms. Black."

"Yes, well, I have to keep a few secrets, don't I?"

Lindsey nodded to Lady Katy. "I'd best get to it before he's too drunk to stand. Don't want to require someone to carry him for me. Good luck with your new toy." Lindsey tugged John's tie as she shifted toward the crowd of dancers. "Come along, Mr. Smith. That's a good boy."

John staggered after her, his back itching from the gaze of Lady Katy. Damn, that woman needed to be put down like a rabid weasel. *And I'd do it if my hands were steady enough.*

Some of his strength had returned as the effects of the drug wore off, but he still remained unsteady and they didn't have much time. The orderlies would be back soon to administer the next dose of drugs and they'd sound the alarm when they found him and Lindsey gone. She must have sensed his unease because she grabbed his hand to pull him closer. He bent his head to her ear and inhaled her lovely scent.

"Which way is out from here?" He had a tough time focusing on anything in the undulating crowd splashed with strobe lighting.

"To your left." He swung them around and eyed her direction. "Under the red light. They try to make it look like there's blood everywhere to keep people from leaving when they're drunk. It's a visceral reaction from what I've seen."

"Hell, that's diabolical." John swallowed against his stomach trying to heave up bile. The tile patterns on the floor seemed to shift like moving entrails in the crimson light. *Just keep your eyes on the prize, Chief.* "Let's move out."

"Roger that."

John blinked and shot her a look, but Lindsey pasted a false smile over her lips and beckoned him with a curling finger as she pulled him toward the doors. Bodies jostled them and made their progress torturous under the shifting lights. John tried to keep moving in a straight line, but his eyes refused to focus and he staggered to his knees, dragging Lindsey down with him.

*Aw shit.*

Lindsey giggled as if completely drunk and bent at the waist, laughing helplessly as she removed her shoes. "Oh my God, you're so drunk." She chortled as she tugged on him. "I gotta get you home, lover."

When John looked up no smile graced her lips and she tensed when a bouncer looked down over her shoulder.

"Everything all right here, miss?"

Lindsey reeled back, rotating her head to an impossible angle. "Hi! Aren't you cute? I'm fine. I'm just trying to help Johnny Boy out the door. He's so drunk." She wobbled and waved her stripper heels in John's direction, smacking him on the shoulder. "Oops, sorry."

"Hey, watch it." His voice came out slurred just as he'd hoped.

The bouncer glowered. "C'mon, buddy. We'll get you out."

John weakly shoved him off and grasped Lindsey's elbow. "I don't need no help. I can walk on my own." He took a few wobbling steps toward the door, dragging Lindsey along with him. She giggled again, but tension tightened her shoulders.

"I'll just help you to your car."

"That's okay. We're staying close by." She leaned in close to the bouncer and gave him a bawdy wink. "I'm gonna show him how a real woman likes it." She hiccoughed and swayed, but kept her feet. "C'mon, Johnny Boy, you promised to show me a good time."

"Yeah, you know I will."

The bouncer hesitated and John's gut tightened, but he smiled his best leer and grabbed Lindsey's ass, squeezing. She squealed and staggered closer to the entrance. The display of drunken love must have convinced the bigger man because he pushed through the crowd to the door and let them out into the heated night.

John followed her, wishing he had greater stability in his movements, but dragging his feet played a more authentic role. Lindsey held on to his arm, swaying as she waited for the bouncer to close the door to the club. When he disappeared inside, she put her shoes back on and led John over to the valet, her strides sure but slow. John scowled. *Dammit, I wish I could keep up with her.*

Despite their methodical progress, Lindsey smiled and waved to one of the valets.

"Good evening, Pedro. Can you get my car, please?"

"Of course, Ms. Black. I see your date has had a little too much fun, eh?"

"Aw, you know how they get when in the Man Cave Club. They just need a little TLC."

"Right. I'll bring your car around, Ms. Black." The handsome young man trotted away and John swallowed a snarl. The little punk had been too familiar with his woman.

*Whoa. Since when is Lindsey my woman?* Nobody had qualified for the title since he'd joined the SEALs three years earlier. No one had been intriguing enough to grab his attention long. Quick fucks and short dalliances. They'd been the extent of his romantic efforts. *But Lindsey's different.* And he wanted more of her.

"You okay, John?" Lindsey laid a gentle kiss on his lips.

"Yeah, ready to be done standing, though."

"Soon. Just need the car. Then you can rest."

Pedro zipped up in a little silver Audi and handed Lindsey the keyless fob as he came around the car.

"There you go, Ms. Black. I made sure it was safe and secure for your date." The young man winked with a sly grin.

"Thanks, Pedro." She handed him a fifty dollar bill and helped John to the passenger side of the car.

"Do you need help to get him in, Ms. Black? He's a

big guy."

"No, we'll be fine. But thanks." Lindsey maneuvered him to the passenger side. "How are you doing? Can you get in on your own?" Her breath brushed his cheek and his cock hardened again. *At least that part of me still works.*

"Yeah." He reached for the car as she pulled the door open.

"Good. Let me recline the seat. When I drive out of here I don't want you too visible." She pushed the leather bucket seat flat. He admired the sleek lines of her dress against her ass and closed his eyes, remembering the softness of it on his lap.

"John, are you okay?"

He snapped his eyes open and nodded, swaying a little.

"Get in and we'll get out of here."

John dropped into the seat with exaggerated movements. Nothing sat where he expected and he banged his knees and forehead twice before he settled into the seat and lay back. God it felt good to relax after trying to walk all that way fighting the ketamine. But they'd made it to the car. All they had to do was get out of the parking lot.

Lindsey settled into the driver's seat and started the engine, the rumble adding to the tremors rippling through his body. *Fuck, I hate coming down off drugs.* The car moved and his sense of orientation shifted, the glow of the Strip's lights washing across the windshield in a kaleidoscope of color.

"Wow. It looks like it's moving. Day and night, always moving."

"Sorry? What's moving?"

"The lights. In Sin City. Did we sin yet?"

Lindsey shot him an incredulous look. "Yep. Plenty of times."

"Good." She looked like a woman good at sinning.

The world spun by the windows, streaks of colored light across shadow, and John let his mind drift. Odd twitches and muscle spasms jolted his body, especially when the car turned. He felt like a beached fish, caught out of the water and gasping for life as his lower extremities faded into numbness. Comfort sat just out of reach, across a console, in a little black dress.

Who was she? *Lindsey.* Lovely, sexy, strong Lindsey who'd come out of nowhere and given him pleasure when the dark closed in on him. *She's my clear water.* Clear water meant safety, a position of strength, and a lull in danger. *She's my home.*

Except the statement seemed inaccurate like an interrogation suspect dodging the truth.

John rolled his head to examine the woman driving beside him as the lights dimmed from garish pinks and whites to more sedate sodium orange. She belonged to him, and yet not. A new gift unclaimed. He wanted her, wanted to keep her, or stay with her. But sluggish memories tugged at his attention, whispering of plans yet unmet.

"Lindsey?"

"Yes, John?"

"Take me home with you."

"I am. You're safe now."

Safety and Lindsey. Perfection.

John let the thickness of his thoughts and the heat of the early summer night suck him down into floating serenity. A weak voice insisted he should be vigilant, always alert to threats, but he shoved it away. His body slowly awakened to sensation, but everything seemed to weigh more than normal. He didn't want to move, and as the car left the lights behind, he allowed his mind to fade into the darkness.

They didn't speak as the pitch of the road changed. *Are we going up?* He cracked his eyes open, but no light came through the windows. Only the dim blue glow of the dash lights offered any definition in the world around him. Discomfort built in his ears and he yawned to relieve the pressure as the car slowed and turned.

The world rattled when the car dropped off pavement and crawled along a gravel road. John squeezed his eyes shut against the shaking, wanting to get off whichever ride they'd strapped him to. When the car came to a stop, the engine shut off and the woman beside him sighed with what sounded like relief. Bronco's opinion mirrored hers. *Thank God the shaking's stopped.* His internal gyroscope warned his head sat lower than his hips, but he only wanted to sleep.

"We're here, John."

He knew that voice. He'd heard the sweet huskiness crying out in pleasure as he thrust into her glorious heat. Had his dream goddess returned?

"Can you open your eyes? We need to get inside where you can sack out all you want."

Yeah, that's what he wanted. Only he wanted her there with him. He wanted to wrap his aching body around her solid warmth and allow it to drag him down into his dreams.

She left him for a moment. As inured to sensation as he'd been, he still noticed when she'd gone, taking her flowery scent with her. Struggling to turn his head, he opened his eyes. Brilliant sodium lights glared through the windshield and made him squint. The car smelled expensive—leather seats?—but not new.

The door beside him opened and his goddess returned. "Come on. Can you still walk?"

"Yes, ma'am." He was a SEAL, dammit. He could damn well do anything.

But his body failed him when he tried to shift it and his legs wobbled like Jell-O in a three-year-old's grip. *What the fuck's wrong with me?*

"Lean on me, John. I've got you." Lindsey worked her shoulder under his armpit and pulled him.

He tipped precariously forward and stared at her feet as

she stabilized his weight. *Where are her shoes? She'll ruin her nylons.* Except she hadn't worn them. He remembered an unencumbered access to her sweet pussy and the satisfaction he'd found there. Warmth ran through his body and hardened his shaft.

"Come on, John. In you go."

She helped him stagger up some rough-hewn plank steps into a clean and homey cabin with wood floors and thread-bare furniture. The walls had been stained golden and glowed in the few lights she'd turned on. The air held the smell of stale air and cool mountain forest. This place didn't seem like something near the Strip in Vegas. Where the hell had she taken him?

Lindsey deposited him on a worn plush couch and made a move away from him. Unreasoning panic exploded in his chest and he grabbed her arm.

"Don't leave me."

"Easy, John. I'm just going to the kitchen to make some coffee. But I won't—"

"Go alone?"

"Be gone long." She patted his arm. "It'll be okay."

He gritted his teeth and nodded. "Just watch your back. They could be anywhere."

"They?"

"The tangos. They can look like anyone. Bartenders, hookers. Hell, that valet you got the car from. Anyone." He had to make her understand. Shadows hid all manner of evils. She had to be careful.

"I'll do another sweep of the cabin, but I'm pretty sure we're clear."

"I should go with you." He struggled to rise.

"No, John. I did a preliminary sweep and came up clear." Lindsey held him still and his traitorous body accepted her direction. "But I'll do another and start the coffee. Stand down, Chief Petty Officer."

"Aye aye, ma'am." The response was automatic. She'd

gotten him out of a bad situation and knew the lay of the land better. He had to trust her.

She nodded and padded silently away. John tried to watch where she went, but the walls hid her form and tension filled his body beneath the wretched tremors shaking him. Time dragged on into infinity and his unease hit a screaming pitch by the time she returned to the room.

"All clear, Chief. I'm going to make coffee. Are you good?"

Lindsey appeared before him still in her cute little black dress and he drank in her sexy form. Damn, the woman could pose for a fashion magazine with that body. He'd only gotten small samples of it, but he wanted more.

"Chief?" Lindsey patted his shoulder and he opened his eyes again.

"Yes, ma'am?"

"Are you good? Can I make the coffee now?"

"Yes, ma'am."

"Do you take anything in it?"

"No, ma'am. Just black."

"Okay. Give me a few minutes. I'm going to start it and bring in the gear."

Gear? He couldn't remember where he'd left his truck or the possessions he'd brought with him from Virginia. Had she found them? Bronco frowned and rubbed the scar along his cheek bone. He'd gotten it from an interrogation in SERE school when he'd met the edge of a metal table with his face. It always helped clear his head to slide his fingers along its rough ridge.

The rich scent of coffee wafted over him as the door to the cabin opened and Lindsey passed him, carrying two duffel bags and her stripper heels. He hadn't gotten a good look at her in those shoes, but he'd bet they made her legs look long and lean. His cock stirred as his imagination kicked into high gear.

Lindsey's warm fruity scent passed him and she

disappeared into a hallway he hadn't noticed. A light came on and the coffee maker chirped from the kitchen. Bronco wished he could get up and pour them both a cup, but he suspected he'd spill it. Rustling sounds drifted from the hallway and after a few minutes, Lindsey returned dressed in a pair of shorts and a black t-shirt that read, "Security for Area 51" across her tits. The fabric stretched taut over her breasts and his cock saluted the curves.

"Give me a second and I'll have coffee for you." Lindsey skimmed her hand up his arm and across his shoulders as she passed.

She rattled around in the kitchen and returned with a steaming cup of coffee. The scent mixed with her sweet fragrance and he swore she offered him candy. She held the cup out to him and miraculously his hands curled around simple white porcelain.

"Got it?"

"Yeah. I think so." John slowly lifted the mug to his lips and sipped. Hot, strong brew slid over his tongue and he hissed as it burned. "Damn, that's good."

"Thanks." Her lovely smile lit her whole face. "I'm kinda a coffee snob. If it's not rich or strong, it's just dirty water."

A chuckle rumbled up from his chest and filled the room with warm sound. He hadn't realized how much he'd missed the sound of his own voice. John had been rather taciturn when with the other SEALs of his squad, but he'd always been able to speak when needed. The forced silence had worn on him and thoughts bounced off the walls of his skull, screaming to escape.

"That's a nice sound." Lindsey settled on the couch beside him with her own mug.

"It's good to be able to make any sound at all." He sipped the coffee to keep from ogling her sweet curves encased in cotton. "Thank you for getting me out."

"You're welcome, John. I'm glad I could help.

Besides, it couldn't have come at a better time."

"Oh, yeah?" He leaned back and rested his head against the couch pillows. "How so?"

"I've been undercover trying to infiltrate that fucked-up sex ring for two years." She shrugged and lines he'd never noticed framed her mouth and eyes. "I was starting to lose myself beneath the psychotic cover persona." She shook her head. "The Black Widow. A woman who prefers her men docile and incapacitated. Shit." She sipped her coffee as if to rid her mouth of a bad taste.

John laid a hand on one of her thighs and squeezed gently. *Damn, she still has plenty of muscle in these sexy legs.* "You aren't your cover persona, Lindsey. You saved me when I couldn't save myself. That's huge. Mistress Jenna the Black Widow would have held me down and let me rot." He met her brown gaze, noting golden sparkles glittering in the warm light. *Beautiful.* "It's not something I like to admit, but without you, I'd be just another body left in the desert for the coyotes. And one thing I learned quick in the Navy: You're nothing without your team."

Lindsey studied him for a few moments, her expression thoughtful. "What was your specialty in the Navy?"

He gave her a half smile. "Interrogation for the SEALs."

Her eyes widened. "You're a SEAL?"

"Yes, ma'am." He took a sip of coffee.

"No wonder you're so beautiful."

He choked and set his mug down as he wiped his face. "Say again?"

Lindsey had the grace to blush. "Sorry. I have a thing for military men and the SEALs are my all-time favorites."

"Oh, yeah?" Her frank words warmed his heart in ways he'd never experienced before. Women often professed a love for SEALs, but it meant more to him coming from Lindsey.

"Yeah, the men in my family have all served. My dad was Army and my uncles elected for the Marines. But the Navy, both the flyboys and the SEALs, have been my favorites."

Old rivalries rose in his chest and curled his lips in a knowing smirk. "Yeah, the Navy pilots have some pretty nice toys, but get 'em on the ground, and they're like fledglings. SEALs go everywhere."

Lindsey laughed. "Yep, they do, and I wouldn't have expected you to tell me different. Very much a SEAL response."

"Sounds like you've had some experience with SEALs before." Bronco reached for his coffee and took a swig.

"Yeah, once or twice. They didn't think much of us, but I could see why. They were saving our asses."

"Now that sounds like an opening for a story."

Lindsey snorted. "Not a very good one. Our platoon got hammered in Fallujah and they had to come rescue the remainder of us. I got to see the aftermath. Brutal stuff, but the SEALs saved the day."

"You're a vet?"

"Yep. Army corpsman, or woman, as is the case."

John's respect for Lindsey hit the roof. She'd gone into civilian law enforcement after her enlistment, and not just any role, but deep undercover. Damn, sexy didn't even begin to describe her.

"I'm impressed, Lindsey. No wonder you're so damn good at your job."

Lindsey snorted. "Come on. You can't mean that. SEALs never say good things about the Army."

"That's not true." He finished his coffee and set the mug down with mock censure. "We're grateful you've done all the grunt work so we can swoop in, clean up the mess, and take all the understated glory." He grinned to take the sting out of his words.

Lindsey laughed like he hoped she would, and rose.

"Do you want some more coffee, hot stuff, or are you set for now?"

"I don't want more coffee. I would like some water, though."

"Roger that. Stand by." She turned toward the kitchen and he grunted.

"It makes sense now."

"What does?"

"Why you respond with military calls. I thought it kinda odd comin' from a civilian, but comin' from a vet like you, it fits."

"Heh, old habits die hard."

She returned and handed him a bottle of water. Condensation laced the plastic surface and slicked his hands, making it difficult to hold. He couldn't grip the lid to twist it off and cursed as the bottle slipped.

"Here, let me get that." She deftly removed the lid and handed the bottle back to him, but his hands shook so much some of it spilled.

"Dammit."

"Crap. I think you're coming down off the drugs and your body's reacting. Let's get the water into you, then get you to bed."

Lindsey settled beside him on the couch and helped him hold the bottle steady at his lips. It galled him to be so weak, but he knew recovery from drugs wouldn't be easy. *And the only easy day was yesterday.*

He swallowed as much of the water as he could before the tremors took over his whole body and even his head wouldn't stay still. Lindsey capped the bottle and set it aside before she stood and offered him her hand.

"Come on, sailor. Let's get you in your rack. Do you think you can still stand?"

"Might be a bit choppy, but I'll make it to the other room."

"Copy that. Lean on me and we'll get you there."

Lindsey offered him resistance to pull him to his feet then ducked under his arm to steady him. Shivers wracked his body and dizziness assailed his head. He groaned and hunched over, giving her more weight than he meant to.

"Easy, bronco. Let's just take it one step at a time."

"Wh-wh-why did y-you c-c-call me th-that?" Damn, his body had grown cold just between sitting and standing.

"'Cause I rode you hard, remember?" He couldn't see her face, but her voice held humor.

"I-it's my n-n-nickname."

"In the SEALs?"

"Yeah."

"Damn, I'm good." She hugged him closer to her side as she half-dragged him down the hallway. "I'll remember that for when I need a pick-me-up when this is over. Something to make me smile when you head off to your team."

An odd sadness sparked in his chest, echoed in her voice as she helped him to the bedroom with red and green plaid curtains over the window. Wood-paneled walls matched the rough pine bole furniture and the worn quilt covering the double bed. She'd added a cheap camping bag on top, but she jerked the quilt back one-handed before she sat him in the bag.

"Okay, Chief, listen to me here. I know you're starting the withdrawal process and it's gonna make you feel weaker than a newborn kitten, but just hold on while I get you undressed. Got me?"

Bronco nodded as Lindsey knelt in front of him and pulled off his shoes. He tried to work on taking off the suit jacket and shirt, but his hands shook so hard he couldn't grasp the buttons. His frustration mounted as he swayed and he had to use his arms to hold himself up.

"Easy, John. I got it. Just be patient." Lindsey's soothing voice settled some of his anger and he closed his eyes. *At least that stops the world from spinning.*

Her deft touches calmed him and he fell into her ministrations. She unbuttoned his shirt and pulled the jacket of each arm in turn, followed by the sleeves of the collared shirt.

"Let's get those pants off you."

John chuckled. "Something a man always likes to hear."

"Very funny, sailor, but I figure you'll be more comfortable in sweats, especially if you get chills."

"Roger that."

She laid him down on the camping bag and worked his pants off. He shivered so hard his cock refused to salute her. He'd reprimand it later for that. In the meantime, she'd already stuffed his feet into a pair of new sweats. The soft fabric slid over his legs, bringing an odd sense of comfort and relaxation to his chilled skin.

"Lift your hips for me, John." Lindsey's hands against his hips and waistline thrilled and comforted him all at once. And he wanted more.

"I have a t-shirt for you too, if you want it."

John opened his eyes and tried to sit up. Lindsey grasped his hand and pulled him upright then handed him the long sleeved tee. He threw it over his head and shrugged it into place then settled back against the camping bag.

Lindsey reached over him and zipped it up, adding the quilt on top. "Snug as a bug in a rug. Sleep tight, John." She laid a soft kiss on his forehead before retreating to the door of the room.

"Lindsey?"

She paused and looked back.

"Thanks for saving me this time. A SEAL's only as good as his team, and you're a damn fine teammate."

"Thanks, John. If you need me, I'll be right across the hall in the other room. Get some sleep."

"Roger that." He ended his words on a yawn and she

chuckled before flipping off the light and pulling the door mostly closed.

John listened to her puttering around the cabin, but his exhaustion pulled him down into the warm and comforting darkness.

# CHAPTER EIGHT

A roar ripped Lindsey out of sleep and had her scrambling for the floor. *Holy fuck! What is that?* Listening around her thundering heart proved problematic until another sound of fury tore through the quiet night. She leapt up and shot across the hall into John's room.

The SEAL thrashed in his bed as if someone held him down and fury filled his expression as he tore at the bedclothes. Damn, he needed help, but she understood about nightmares and soldiers who'd experienced traumatic events. Getting close to him could be hazardous for her health.

Lindsey bit her lip and scanned the room. A small lamp sat on the bureau across from the bed and she switched it on. The soft light warmed the room without blinding her and she returned to the bed. *Gotta get his attention without adding to the nightmare.*

Taking a deep breath to calm herself down, Lindsey knelt on the floor far enough from the bed he wouldn't hit her if he flailed. *Gotta be calm, just like Mom was when Dad came back shell-shocked from Vietnam. Can't believe I'm using this now.*

"John, I'm here for you. It's Lindsey. Can you hear

me?"

She waited, hoping her voice would reach through to whatever hell he thrashed in. She didn't dare touch him yet, not until she knew he recognized her. John froze in the bed, his breathing rough, but his body language cautious.

"I don't know where you are right now, but physically your body is here with me at the safe house and you're secure." Lindsey kept her voice calm and even, praying she'd reach him. She wanted to wrap him in her arms and tell him everything was okay, but that hadn't always worked with her father. "Are you reading me, Chief Petty Officer?"

Sometimes her mother had gotten through by using her father's rank. The military training went deep and anchored soldiers in something familiar. Lindsey remembered the frightening times her father had lost it and how her mother had kept them all from panicking by staying calm. *I owe you one, Mom. I promise to call and thank you when I get out of this undercover shit.*

"Chief?"

"Roger that." John's breathless voice reached her despite its softness.

"Good, Chief. I'm right here. Right beside you and you're not restrained, but I can help get the blankets off you." She didn't move, watching his body. "Do you need me to move the blankets?"

Seconds ticked by recorded only by her heartbeats. She resisted the urge to rip the covers away and hold him. *I'll be dead before I can get close.* He had too much training in hand-to-hand and regret only came after safety was attained.

"Are we secure?"

"We're secure, John. Can I take your hand? Would that help ground you?" Lindsey locked her arms to her sides and forced herself to wait.

"How do I know you're the real Lindsey?" He didn't

have to tell her he worried her cover had been blown.

Lindsey took a deep breath and thought back to the conversations they'd had in private.

"I know your nickname is Bronco and you're a US Navy SEAL. I told you I'm a coffee snob when you said you prefer your coffee black, and I'm a US Army vet." Lindsey paused for breath. She suspected she'd missed a few other details, but she didn't want to waste time. "I know you were on a PCS when you stopped in Vegas for some R&R, and your specialty is interrogation. All these details ringing true, Bronco?"

John didn't say anything, but his body hadn't relaxed yet, the muscles in his neck standing out against the skin like organic ropes. *He really is beautiful even when he's liable to kill me.* She wished he'd verify her responses quickly, but her mother always said patience was key and they had to stand strong when her father couldn't. *Gotta be strong for John now.*

"Lindsey?"

"Yes, John?"

"I can't see anything clearly. The shadows are shifting around too much."

"I'm right beside the bed, John. If I have your permission, I can free your hand and hold it."

"Permission granted."

Lindsey exhaled the breath she didn't know she'd been holding and reached for the tangled blankets. "This is me, John. I'm pulling back the covers to give you more range of motion." She kept her voice even as she tugged the camping bag away from his body. Sweat soaked his shirt and matted his hair, but he held perfectly still. "I'm going to free your whole body so anything you feel around your legs or hips is just me. I'm right here, John."

She kept tugging at the blankets and when she freed his torso and legs, she returned to the side of the bed and grasped his hand.

"I've got you, John. I'm holding your hand. Can you see anything better yet?"

"No."

"Okay. I'm right here. Do you need me to shut up or keep talking?" Sometimes her father had needed silence. Sometimes he'd needed her mother's soothing voice. Back then no one had a name for Post Traumatic Stress Disorder, but Marian Jarvis had instinctively known how to deal with it. Her husband had been able to face life at home because of her.

"Please talk to me." For all John's stillness, his body lay rigid with tension and his hand closed tightly around hers.

"Okay, John. I told you my dad was in the Army, right?" John nodded. "He got drafted for Vietnam and when he came home he had what they called shell-shock back then. Nobody had a name for PTSD. It was a big surprise when he'd get angry over me or my sister dropping things or making loud noises. He hated the fireworks on the Fourth of July or New Year's, and he started avoiding family gatherings and large crowds."

Lindsey could still picture her father's white face every time a car backfired.

"At first, none of us knew what to do. My sister and I were too little to really understand anything other than dad was just angry all the time. But my mom, she was pretty special." A smile curled Lindsey's lips at the memory of her tall, slender mother facing down the bear her father had become. She'd shown patient determination to protect their children from his overwhelming ferocity. "She somehow knew what to do to bring back the man she'd married. She knew how to reconnect with him even before doctors and psychologists understood what PTSD was."

John's body slowly relaxed as Lindsey talked, his breathing slowing. "This was back in the 1970's and I was just a little kid, but some of my friends' parents blamed the soldiers for the war. I used to come home crying because my friends told me my daddy was a baby killer. I was only four." Anger rumbled in her gut for the injustice her dad had gone through. "It still pisses me off to this day. It wasn't their choice to go overseas. Some of them didn't even get a choice about joining the Army. My mom caught all sorts of shit from the hippie peace movement for being married to and supporting a veteran, but I can definitely say she knew more about making love than most of them ever did. She never spewed hate and she never attacked anyone for choosing to stay home for peace or go off to war. She was amazing."

"Is your mom still alive?" John's whisper brought Lindsey back to the present.

"I think so. I haven't seen her or my dad for over two years." Tears threatened to build up as sorrow filled her chest. *God, I'm so ready to be done undercover.* She hadn't realized how much she missed her family until now. "I had to cut all personal ties when I went undercover."

"I'm sorry, Lindsey. Family is important." John sounded more settled as if some of the demons had faded.

"You're right, which is why I want out of this gig. But I don't regret taking this assignment. It gave me a chance to meet you." Lindsey stopped before she said more. *Damn, girl, are you falling for this guy? You hardly know him.*

John snorted. "You count meeting me as a good thing?"

Lindsey weighed her responses. "Meeting you is a good thing. The circumstances surrounding that meeting? Not on my list of favorites."

He grunted with what sounded like amusement. "I think I would've chosen a different setting to meet you, too. But I'm glad you were there."

She tried not to read too much into his words. *Relax, he's just grateful you got him out. There's nothing more to it.* But her heart wanted to do a very girly happy dance over it.

"Are you feeling a little better?" She rubbed the back of his hand in gentle circles with her thumbs. "Do you need any water?"

"I'd like some water, but I don't want you to let go." His hand tightened on hers.

"I won't let go, John. I promise." She sighed and leaned back against the small bedside table. Not the most comfortable position, but she refused to release John's hand. "I'll be right here as long as you need me."

"I need you, Lindsey. Could you lie down next to me on the bed?" John's jaw clenched and he swallowed hard. "It'll be easier to fall asleep if I can feel you beside me. I just need to know you're here with me. If you're here, I know I'm secure."

His level of trust in her struck Lindsey momentarily dumb. She'd once asked her dad how he'd climbed out of the hole of PTSD. He'd told her it all came down to trusting her mother to let him know when the bad stuff he thought he saw was actually real. If she remained calm, he knew he didn't have to fight. To be given that level of trust from John humbled Lindsey.

"Of course I can, John." She rolled to her feet without releasing his hand. "I'm going to let go of your hand just long enough to turn off the light and walk around the bed. It shouldn't take me more than ten seconds. Okay?"

"Roger that." Tension bled into his voice, but he let go of her hand.

Lindsey wasted no time turning off the lamp and returning to the bed. She lifted the quilt and the camping bag to slide in beside him, trying to keep her motions smooth.

"It's me, Chief." She grasped his hand and squeezed. "I'm right beside you in the bed. See?" She snuggled up to his sweat-soaked body. "Soft and real breasts, remember?"

A chuckle rumbled up from John's chest. "I still

haven't seen them in person, but I remember how they feel."

"Good. I have them right here." She squirmed a little against him, pressing her breasts to his side. "Try to get some sleep, John. I'll let you know if there's anything to be worried about. Ten-four?"

"Copy that." His voice sounded sleepy. "Thank you, Lindsey."

"You're welcome." She smiled. "Good night, sleep tight, don't let the bedbugs bite."

His tired chuckle warmed her heart as she held his body close.

# CHAPTER NINE

The next two days were an exercise in patience and endurance. In her more humorous moments, Lindsey wondered if she'd run into her own version of Hell Week. John swung from episodes of delirium to whole hours of lucidity. The lucidity allowed her to get to know him, but when the shakes would take him, his frustration at his weakness overrode everything else, she could only hold on for the ride.

In a quiet moment when John needed space the day after they arrived, Lindsey found time to text Courtney their situation report.

*Hey, Courtney. Date went well, but lost the phone over the dam. It was a wild time. Picked up the cutest Armani dress and hung it in the closet. It wasn't on sale but it needs some cleaning so can't wear it right away. How are you? Jenna.*

Lindsey scrubbed her hands over her face. *Damn right, he needs some cleaning.* The ketamine messed with John's mind on the recovery, and his nightmares had been horrific. She'd held him through most of them, talking to him to keep him anchored in the present. *And to keep him from killing me.*

Her phone chirped with an incoming text. *Damn, girl, where have you been? I was worried. Glad to hear date went well. Sucks about phone. Was the dress damaged?*

*Define damaged.* Lindsey sighed and typed out her new message. *No, just needs a good cleaning. When it's ready, I'll show you. Maybe I'll bring my date by and you can meet him. Oh, and tell the Old Man of the Sea that next week's plans are still good.*

She hoped Courtney understood she meant the Navy. They expected John in Coronado a week from Monday and she figured they could get him free of the detox by then.

*Will do. BTW, I found a sleek and sexy truck that Bill coveted. I'll text pics to this number so you can show your date when you see him again. I bet he'll recognize the make and model.* So Courtney had found John's truck. *See you Monday for a run?*

Lindsey shook her head. *No, I have plans, but Weds latest. Will show my date the pics. Can hardly wait to see them. :)*

Instead of a response, Courtney sent her two text photos and she scanned the sleek silver quarter-ton pickup with a topper. It showed signs of travel, but looked in great condition and screamed John all the way.

Lindsey typed back a short reply then rose as she heard John moan from the bedroom in the back. Demons came at all hours and she'd promised to help him fight them. *Even when they're almost as scary as my dad's.*

By Tuesday morning, John's episodes of delirium and shakes had stopped, and he could easily move around by himself. He'd taken a few runs around the deer trails behind the cabin for PT, and Lindsey tried to pretend she didn't enjoy it when he walked in the door and ripped his shirt off on the way to the shower. She hadn't touched him intimately since the last night at the hotel, and chafed under the irony of missing it.

*It was just part of the job, Jarvis. He needs friendship and professionalism more than sexual release...dammit.*

When he returned to the kitchen, the sun glinted off his wet hair as he scrubbed the towel over his head. She inhaled the scents of vanilla and sandalwood from the shampoo she'd bought as he walked up to where she leaned over an old sci-fi book she'd found on the shelves.

"Did you make coffee?" The heat from his body warmed her skin as he stood close.

"Yeah. There's a whole fresh pot over there."

He strode to the coffee maker and she surreptitiously watched his ass all the way. Beads of water dotted his back and sparkled like fairy dust as his muscles flexed when he poured a cup. *Oh, now you're just waxing teenaged-girl. Your focus needs focus, Jarvis.*

Lindsey yanked her attention back to her book when John turned and sat down across the table from her.

"What are you reading?"

She couldn't even remember, not with that gloriously hairy chest across from her. "Um." She flipped the cover over. "Some science fiction story. It's okay. How was your run today?"

"Better. I'm still slow, but fifty-five hundred feet might give anyone trouble." John frowned and sipped his coffee.

Lindsey gasped and covered her mouth with one hand in dramatic surprise. "A SEAL admitting the elevation gave him trouble?"

A sexy grin curled John's lips at her ribbing. "Hey, now, don't you go repeatin' that to anyone, hear? I gotta preserve my reputation as a badass."

She laughed and closed the book. "Well, I think you're badass to have come out of this so well. You should be ready to head in tomorrow."

He sobered and tipped his head. "Head in?"

"Yeah, for a debriefing with Metro PD. We've been

working on this case against Madame LeBeau for five years now, and I've been on it for two. They need what you know as an insider." She shook her head. "With the information I've brought, you're the link they need to bring the bitch down." Her hand tightened around her mug. "She needs to be locked away forever."

"You won't get an argument from me." He scanned her face for long, thoughtful moments. "What will you do now, Lindsey? I'm sure your cover is shot to hell by getting me out. What's ahead for you?"

She inhaled long and slow, enjoying his scent along with the coffee. "I'm going to chop my hair off so it's easily maintained, I'm going to let the dye grow out of it, and I'm going to take an ordinary detective job, like sex crimes or homicide. I'm done with undercover work." She met his gaze. "I want to see my family, and have real friends, not just my handler. I want to talk to my mom and tell her how amazing she was while I was growing up. She not only held the family together, but took care of my dad in a way the psych docs hadn't even discovered yet." She smoothed the mug's handle with her fingers. "I want to see my sister, my dad, and my uncles, and remember what it's like to have a family that cares around me."

Lindsey bit off her stream of words before they went straight into hysterics. She hadn't realized just how tired of the game she'd become.

"Sorry. Helping you through the last few days showed me what I've been missing and how far I've gone into loneliness and isolation. I didn't mean to dump it all on you."

"Don't apologize, Lindsey." John peeled one of her hands off her mug and held it in his callused palm. "God knows I've been dumping my shit on you this whole time, and I couldn't have gotten through most of it without you." He snorted and shrugged, but never released her hand. "Hell, don't tell anyone, but I think of you as my knight in sexy armor. The Navy put me through hell in hopes it would prepare me for any situation they could imagine, and all the ones they couldn't." He shook his head. "But all that training didn't do shit when my body wasn't mine to control. A SEAL's only as strong as his team, and I'd have you on my team in an op like that anytime."

John rose and cupped her face with his rough hands. "If I haven't told you yet, thank you for getting me out and being here when I detoxed." He brushed his lips across hers and fierce yearning for more burned in her chest.

*You can't have more. He's a Navy SEAL headed for his duty in Coronado and you're a cop in Vegas. Let him go, Jarvis.* But her heart screamed with fury over the loss of something so fragile, she couldn't give it a name. *I won't call it love. I can't call it love.*

Her hands gripped his wrists of their own accord and she opened her mouth just as his tongue brushed her lips for entrance. Lindsey moaned as she sank into his kiss. He sidled closer, pressing the hard ridge of his erection against her thigh. The solid mass of his flesh through the cloth excited her and she rubbed her leg over the bulge.

Searing-hot lust slammed into her and she met the thrust of his tongue with her own. He growled and slid his hands into her hair, angling her head to settle into their kiss. Vanilla spice filled her nose as he pulled her against his chest. Her gut tightened and her pussy spasmed. *Holy shit this man can kiss.*

John pulled back and panted, his forehead pressed against hers. "Lindsey, I want to thank you properly. Would you let me?"

"What's your definition of a proper thank you?"

"I'm going to take you into the bedroom and kiss you all over."

"All over?" Did her voice just squeak?

"Yes, ma'am. All over. Will you let me?"

"Hoorah, Chief."

"Hooyah, ma'am."

He dipped to pick her up and carried her like an old movie heroine into the bedroom where she'd held him through his nightmares. He laid her on the camping bag and tugged at her jean shorts until they slid off her hips.

"Oh, nice. Commando." John's sultry smile wetted her nether lips. "I've wanted to taste you since you rode me the other night." He dropped her shorts on the floor and knelt beside the bed. "I could smell your pussy, but I couldn't get close to it. Now I want to savor you and say thanks."

"You know I was doing my duty to serve and protect."

He smiled up at her as he settled her knees against his shoulders. "And it's my duty to acknowledge your efforts and serve you in kind." He dipped his head and brushed his lips over her mound. "Let me thank you, Lindsey. Let me show you my full gratitude."

John's tongue swept her clit and Lindsey saw stars. Pleasure sizzled throughout her body as he continued his sensual onslaught, his tongue dipping between her folds. Slick heat tickled her nether lips and John's rough palms skimmed her hips.

When he burrowed his tongue in her labia, Lindsey whimpered and squirmed in his grip. "Oh, my God, John."

He hummed with amusement, but didn't stop his ministrations. He sucked her clit into the hot cavern of his mouth and squeezed her ass with one hand before tickling her entrance with his finger. Lindsey keened a wail as he slowly teased her, sucking harder on her nubbin.

Fiery pleasure burned a path straight to her head as he thrust his finger into her pussy, rubbing the inner walls. She squirmed harder as he licked her pussy lips with long, measured strokes, matching the thrust of his finger to every swipe. Her orgasm built with each motion until the pad of his finger scraped over her pleasure spot and her arousal caught fire.

"Oh, John. Oh, yes. Yes!"

Lindsey clenched her fists in his hair as he sucked harder on her clit and sped up the thrusts of his finger. He hummed against her nether lips and scrubbed her G-spot until she shot into her release with a scream.

John pulled his head back while he pumped his hand in her clenching slit and crooned, "That's it, Lindsey. Come for me." He pressed his mouth to her clit and stoked the fires as she soared.

At last she settled back down to the world she knew and John crawled up her body to gather her into his arms. It had been years since a man had given her cunnilingus, and longer still since one had done it well. John cradled her against his chest and kissed the side of her head, her own scent mixing beautifully with his vanilla spice.

"Thank you for rescuing me, Lindsey." His whisper warmed her as much as the heat from his body.

*I should be thanking him for eating me out so wonderfully.* But she couldn't find her voice in the flood of endorphins swamping her. She settled for nuzzling her face into his chest, enjoying the scent of his skin and the tickle of his hair. *I need to sleep with my teddy bear more often.*

Too bad this bear couldn't stay and bring her comfort forever.

"You're welcome, John. More than welcome."

They said nothing more and Lindsey drifted toward slumber, trying to shove away the knowledge that tomorrow, he'd be gone.

# CHAPTER TEN

John settled the "I heart Las Vegas" t-shirt over his shoulders and buckled the belt on his jeans. They sat a little low on his hips and bagged around the thighs, but they'd do until he got his truck and gear back. He carried the duffle bag Lindsey had brought for him into the living room and set it beside hers as she wiped down the counters in the kitchen.

"Ready?" she asked.

"Yeah. I got everything out of the room and made the bed."

"With hospital corners, I'm sure."

"Is there any other way?" He grinned as she laughed. "I'm gonna load the last of the gear into the car."

"Thanks. I'm just finishing up here."

John nodded and ignored the oddly comforting feeling of the domestic existence they'd shared for a few days. The detox had been painful, but Lindsey's presence had dulled the edges and soothed the excessive agony. He wanted more domestic bliss with her. *Let it go, Andrews. You gotta get to Coronado.*

He shoved the disappointment deep and threw the bags into the trunk of the car. Lindsey appeared on the steps, locked the door, and hid the key under one of the rocks in a flowerbed beside them. She turned and scanned the gravel road behind the car, sighing. He turned to follow her gaze and listened hard, expecting the sound of an engine or a helo. Only the breeze through the pines met his ears.

"Everything good?"

"Yeah, we're good." The brief smile she gave him didn't light her eyes as she unlocked the doors to the car and got in.

"Thanks for bringing me here. Best safe house I've ever stayed in." John buckled his seat belt as she started the engine.

"Me, too. It helps that no one knows about it except me."

"And now me."

"Right."

They didn't say anything more as she drove them back into Vegas. John settled into his thoughts, turning a blind eye to the world passing outside the windows. He'd have to say goodbye to Officer Lindsey Jarvis and get back to his duty as a SEAL. It should be enough. The adventure, the duty, all his actions centering on changing the world for the better. *Just like Lindsey's doing here.*

But as they pulled into the underground parking structure of the Las Vegas Metro PD, the words felt hollow and cold. He wanted more. *Let it go, Andrews. A SEAL's life is too fluid to have a long-term commitment.* He spent most of his time away, doing things he couldn't talk about to anyone. *She deserves better than that. Really.*

"Ready?"

"Yeah. I'm good." As good as could be expected.

They left the gear in the trunk and took the elevator up to the first floor of the station. Lindsey's body straightened into what John thought of as 'official business' mode and by the time they stepped out into the foyer, she'd become all cop. He donned his patented SEAL mask and followed her past the front desk.

"Hey, Jarvis. Long time no see." The booking sergeant smoothed his hand over his bald scalp as his gaze slid over Lindsey's V-necked shirt and capris. "You here for Dabner?"

John swallowed the growl burning in his chest. *She's not mine so I can't get twitchy about some jackass drooling over her.* He'd drooled over her at a distance, but not in her face. *Have some class, asshole.*

"Yeah, she's expecting me." Lindsey returned the man's stare with a look John described as "unstable awareness." She didn't smile, she didn't frown. She simply stared at the desk sergeant, acknowledging him without emotion.

The man sat back a little and swallowed hard then sneered. "Who's that you got with you, Jarvis?"

"A witness, Schroder. Are you gonna let us pass or what?" Lindsey signed her name on the check-in sheet.

"He's gotta sign in." The desk sergeant scowled as he pointed at John.

"No, he doesn't. Not until Dabner sees him. Then you'll get your paperwork just the way you like it." Lindsey leveled the man with her soulless expression.

"You can't just waltz in here after two years and think the protocols don't apply to you." He leered a greasy smile at Lindsey, flexing his front desk power.

John resisted rolling his eyes.

Lindsey didn't react, just pulled out her phone and tapped a message into the screen. The desk sergeant's smile slowly faded as she ignored him. Within seconds, the front-line phone rang and he picked up the hand set.

"Schroder." His face creased into a scowl. "Yes, ma'am, they're here…No, ma'am, but—" Schroder clenched his jaw. "Yes, ma'am. Will do." He hung up the phone and leveled some ferocious stink-eye at Lindsey. "Guess you're clear to head back."

"Guess so." Her expression never changed as she marched past the desk into the offices beyond.

John followed her, swallowing a smirk. *Damn, she's hot.* He had to hand it to her. She'd learned how to put men in their places after her time in Madame LeBeau's realm.

More than one set of eyes followed them as they made their way to the offices in the back. The whole place smelled like sweat, frustration, and gun oil. Not exactly an armory, but enough weapons rode the hips of the inhabitants to create a distinctive smell.

"Jarvis, good to see you." A tall woman with blond hair and the body of a supermodel grasped Lindsey's hand and shook it, her gaze falling on John. "Glad you made it in. Is this your witness?"

"Yes, Courtney. This is Chief Petty Officer John Andrews." Lindsey shifted her gaze to his and she raised her chin with a proprietary smile. "Let's go to a more private place to discuss the case. There's a lot we can tell you."

Courtney gestured to one of the windowed rooms behind her. Lindsey nodded and led the way. John found a seat in one of the relatively uncomfortable chairs at the table. Lindsey sat beside him and Courtney took the seat across from them.

"All right, Jarvis. Let's get tape on this. Chief Petty Officer Andrews, my name is Detective Courtney Dabner, and anything you can tell me about the inner workings of Madame LeBeau's sex-slave industry will help us make our case against her."

John and Lindsey spent the next four hours relating everything they'd learned in the last week of his incarceration at the hands of Madame LeBeau. Lindsey filled in the holes to John's story and they told a diabolical tale of abduction, drug intoxication, forced prostitution, and murder. The damning evidence would put LeBeau and her cronies away for at least a century. Lindsey knew most of the heavy players and investors, while John described the way the victims were gathered and a few of the women who pulled them in.

Curiously, the name of the sexy, sultry woman he'd met the first time he woke up in Madame LeBeau's dungeon never came up. He filed that away to ask Lindsey later. *If there is a later with her.* The thought sank his gut, but he ignored it. Duty first.

At last, they had covered everything they could think of and Courtney stacked her notes with her phone and a satisfied smile. "Thank you, Chief Petty Officer. This will help us nail this bitch and take her down."

"Anything I could do. You have to give most of the credit to Detective Jarvis, though." John glanced at Lindsey with a smile. "She was the one who found me and pulled me out. She's a damn good undercover detective and I was lucky she had my back."

"Sex crimes detective."

"What?" He and Lindsey spoke at the same time.

"Sex crimes, Chief Petty Officer. The paperwork went through today, as a matter of fact." Lindsey gasped and Courtney nodded with satisfaction. "Yep. As of this morning, you've been assigned a desk. Congratulations, Jarvis." She grinned and shook her head. "HR will be contacting you to fill out the necessary paperwork as soon as you can."

They all stood and John held out his hand to Lindsey. "Well done, Detective Jarvis. Congratulations on your new job. Guess this means you won't be undercover anymore."

"Yeah." Her smile was tinged with disbelief.

"We have also found your truck and secured your gear, Chief. If you'll follow me, we can do the paperwork to have it released to you."

"Thank you, Detective Dabner. I'm glad it could be recovered." He followed the women back into the main squad room.

"Let's get you squared away and you'll be free to go. I believe Coronado is expecting you by Monday?"

"Yes, ma'am." He nodded then paused. "That is, if it's still June. Time didn't have much meaning when under the drugs."

"It's still June, Chief." Lindsey handed him a clipboard with several forms on it. "I made sure to get you out with plenty of time to spare." Though her face held a smile, her gaze seemed unfocused and her voice held distance.

John suppressed a shiver against the loss of intimacy as he signed the forms releasing his property back to him. *It's for the best. I have my duty in Coronado and she's been promoted to detective, just like she wanted.* The logic held strong, but it didn't fix the disappointment dogging its steps.

"Thank you for that, Detective Jarvis."

Her smile broadened with the new title and gave him a measure of pleasure as he handed the clipboard to Dabner.

"Thanks again for sending Jarvis to me. She did a remarkable job undercover as well as getting me out safely." He glanced at Lindsey before returning his gaze to Dabner. "Not that my recommendation means much, but if she ever needs a reference for commendation, I'd be happy to give mine."

Dabner raised her eyebrows. "High praise coming from an operator of your experience, Chief Andrews."

"Yes, ma'am. Detective Jarvis deserves it, ma'am." John didn't mind admitting it. *I'd take her as a teammate anytime.* "A hell of an investigator and undercover agent. She'd do well in SpecOps if the military let women in the front lines."

Lindsey's eyes had grown wide and a blush stained her cheeks, but John meant what he said. It was unlikely women would ever be in the SEALs, but she had the skills to rival any CIA agent he'd encountered.

"Thank you, Chief."

"I'll note that in her file for future reference, Chief. Thanks for the tip." Dabner handed him his keys and gestured toward a side entrance to the building. "Your truck and gear are in the secured garage through that door." She held out her hand to shake and he took it. "Glad you made it out safe and are on your way. Your statements will bring this system down hard and LeBeau won't be getting up or out anytime soon."

"Will I be called to testify later?" John didn't believe he'd be free to do so, but he wanted to check.

"Probably, Chief. While your statements are damning, due process requires your presence. When the time comes, the DA will be in contact with your unit." She looked him up and down with consideration. "I don't think anyone will be coming after you. That's not their style. They seem to go after only local fish."

"Wouldn't matter if they did." One thing he knew: if LeBeau sent someone after him, they'd learn the hard truth about the adage, 'Mess with the best and die like the rest.' "They'd have a whole mess of trouble getting to me and would be liable to meet the business end of a weapon if they did."

"Yep. Good luck and safe journey, Chief Petty Officer."

"Thank you, ma'am."

Dabner retreated to her desk and Lindsey pulled him toward the door to the garage, her body language emanating professional and distant courtesy. John understood the why behind it, but still ached for the loss of their connection.

They stepped through the door and into the sultry heat of the garage. Even though it sat shaded, the summer temperatures of Las Vegas filled the space with rippling warmth and John thanked God he'd worn a t-shirt. Lindsey said nothing as she checked the receipt he'd been given for the location of his truck.

"There it is." She pointed as she strode for the silver pickup and he enjoyed the flex of her ass in her capris as he inhaled the scents of baking motor oil and hot metal. He certainly wouldn't miss the oven heat of Vegas when he left.

But he'd miss Lindsey's sexy heat.

*Let her go. She's got a life now.*

Lindsey paused at the truck and looked up at him, her gaze full of conflicting emotions and thoughts. He couldn't read them. He didn't know her well enough yet. *Yet? You won't get the chance, Andrews.*

"Here you go, Chief. I wish you good luck, fair skies, and clear water. May the wind be always at your back and your sails full." She held out her hand.

John wanted to take her hand and pull her into his arms, holding her for one last time, but he respected her professional façade. He squeezed her palm gently and shook it before unlocking the door.

"That's a helluva blessing you gave. Kinda mixed things, didn't you?"

Lindsey laughed. "Yeah, but my grandfather always said blessings don't have to be said the same as long as they're meant from the heart." She sobered and sincerity filled her expression. "I wish you the best of luck, Chief. And—" She stopped, shaking her head. "No, just luck."

"Thank you, Detective Jarvis. I'll give you the one my grandmother used to say to us." He held both her hands and looked into her eyes. "May you have walls for the wind and a roof for the rain, and drinks beside the fire. Laughter to cheer you and those you love near you, and all that your heart may desire." Unexpected emotion tightened the muscles around his eyes and made his nose tingle. The Celtic blessing suddenly meant more than he thought. "Thanks for all your help."

He released her and climbed into his truck before he did something stupid like kiss her and hold her against his chest. *Just let her go.* He closed the door and rolled down the window, trying to find his patented relaxed smile. It seemed elusive.

"Hey, Bronco." She leaned her arms on the truck door. "I won't tell you to be careful because that's not your job. But be as safe as your profession allows, okay? I like knowing the world still contains the hottest ride I've ever had."

Her face showed professional flippancy, but her eyes shuttered and he found he couldn't read her at all. *Damn, the woman would make a good SEAL.*

"It was a helluva ride. Thanks again, Detective."

"Safe trip, Chief."

He started the truck and threw it into gear, backing away from her. *This is for the best. I'm starting a new duty station and don't have time for anything.* The words didn't have the conviction he would've liked. *She has a new life, too. Clean break is best.*

John drove out of the parking garage pretending his heart didn't ache with each yard and he didn't watch until she disappeared behind the walls of concrete behind him.

# CHAPTER ELEVEN

Lindsey put the finishing touches on the last report for the closed case and sat back in her chair, rubbing her eyes. Damn, she'd forgotten all the paperwork it took when she was in the visible world. When she'd been undercover, her handler had taken care of all of it. *Wouldn't mind her doing that again.*

Courtney no longer oversaw Lindsey's work. She had a new undercover cop to direct and Lindsey knew they had a few cases going on the Strip. *Ah, Vegas. Always a hotbed of people trying to live the 'what happens in Vegas stays in Vegas.' Too bad the cops notice.* Courtney might no longer be her boss, but they'd kept their friendship alive. Even after three weeks since John "Bronco" Andrews drove out of her life, the woman checked up on her.

*I don't miss him.* Lindsey couldn't miss him. She hadn't known him long enough. *Plus, he's a SEAL based in California, when he's home at all.* All good reasons to let him go and move on with her life. *I have the job I want and the time I need to just be normal. So why can't I?*

She'd made a few strides in getting a new life. She'd managed to call her mother and reconnect with her family. Lindsey had choked up so many times on the phone she'd barely been able to speak through her tears. But her mother had invited her to visit them in Reno in their new house for the weekend. Lindsey had made the trip twice.

She rolled her head on her shoulders to loosen them and checked the clock. Weird to think she could just go home at the end of a work day. *Home.* She'd returned to the apartment Metro had kept for her, but it felt like someone else's place. It didn't even smell right. It held all sorts of things she remembered, but none of it felt like it should belong to her, even after three weeks of living there.

Nothing here felt right.

"Hey, you done for the day?"

Lindsey looked up and nodded at Courtney as the tall woman paused at her desk. "Yeah, I was just getting my purse to head out. Nice of the department to let me keep the one I used from my last assignment. It's a bit more expensive than I would've bought myself, but it's pretty." She hefted the burnt sienna Louis Vuitton handbag and slung it over her shoulder.

"They would've just thrown it out and it seems like a waste of good money." Courtney shrugged. "Besides, it looks good on you. Do you have plans for the weekend?"

"Yeah, I have a date with my elliptical and a good book. Not quite as glamorous as when I hung out at all the clubs, but I no longer have the bankroll for that kind of life." Lindsey walked around her desk and headed for the bank of elevators to the parking garage. "What about you?"

"I was hoping you'd agree to go out for a drink with me. You know, blow off the glitter of the work week." Courtney smirked as she pressed the down button.

Lindsey snorted. "I don't know if I'd be good company right now. Still trying to find my equilibrium after returning to the 'real world'. Nothing feels settled or right, you know?"

They stepped into the elevator as Courtney nodded. "Yeah, but that's what I'm here for. Since I know you in both lives, I'm that cornerstone, the keystone, the linchpin. Choose your metaphor."

Lindsey laughed as the car dropped smoothly to the garage and opened. "Yeah, okay. Fine. Where did you want to go?"

"Follow me to Bailey's?" Courtney clicked her fob and her car chirped a few spaces from Lindsey's.

"Yeah. That works. See you there."

Lindsey didn't really want to go out, but it'd be good to reconnect with Courtney. She missed the regular meetings and camaraderie they'd shared while undercover. Somehow she needed to find her feet. She felt like a space alien wandering around trying to find Area 51.

Courtney had already arrived at the bar when Lindsey stepped through the thick doors. Classic rock and roll music enveloped her as she picked her way to Courtney's table, ignoring the scent of cigarette smoke. She shoved away memories of her undercover work and sat down.

"Want a beer?"

Lindsey shook her head. "Not tonight. Gonna take a raspberry iced tea and call it good."

"Aw, you're no fun." Courtney mock-pouted and Lindsey swallowed a snarl.

"You're right. I'm not fun. I don't know how to have fun since the last time I went out for a party I had to watch what I said and did, and pretend I enjoyed sexually debasing men." Lindsey rubbed her forehead. "See? I told you I wouldn't be good company."

"Yeah, I figured, but I had to get you someplace I could talk to you and light a fire under your ass."

Lindsey blinked. "What?"

"Listen, Jarvis. You've been on the job now for two years straight and you haven't had a break from it." Courtney leveled her with a hard stare, her mouth sealing shut as the waitress brought their drinks. She waited with a gentle smile until the woman drifted away, but her eyes remained hard. "You've earned, what, something like a hundred and sixty hours of vacation time? I bet you're at 'use-or-lose' and you're still here working." She shook her head and pointed one manicured nail at Lindsey. "Go away. Take a vacation. Go relax. Visit family again. Do something, because you're a nasty, snarly bitch right now, and that's fun for no one."

"Damn, sugar coat it, why don't you?"

"No point." Courtney fixed her with a stern glare. "You don't need coddling, you need to figure out who the hell you are. A vacation would do you good. Hell, a stay-cation would improve things."

"That's the problem, isn't it?" Lindsey inhaled the scent of stale beer and old cigarette smoke. "I don't know who I am because I've been someone else for two years. And now I'm supposed to be Detective Lindsey Jarvis of sex crimes, but she's so new, I don't know who that is, either. The only time I kinda knew myself, I was hiding in a safe house with Chief Petty Officer John Andrews."

"Then go find him and find yourself while you're at it." Courtney punctuated her words with a sharp nod and a swallow of beer.

"I can't go find him. He's a SEAL, remember? Masters of being unseen, unheard, and deadly?" Lindsey snorted. "He could be standing behind you and I'd never know it."

Courtney twisted around and scanned the bar. "Is he behind me?"

Lindsey thumped her shoulder. "Shut up. You know what I mean."

"No, I don't. He's only been there for three weeks. He's probably getting up to speed with both his new squad and recovering from the shit he experienced here." Courtney pointed to the front door of the bar. "You should go out there to Coronado and request his ass, and shag him for real this time."

"Damn, you're crass." Lindsey grimaced around her

iced tea. "We barely know each other. I can't just show up on his doorstep and say, 'hi, I know we only had a few days together, but I thought we had a connection and so I decided to invade your space. M'kay?'" She shook her head. "He's a SEAL and has to be there. I'm a detective with Metro and have to be here."

"I'm not suggesting you marry him, Jarvis. I'm saying to go out there, get laid, and take a vacation with someone you know is hot and sexy." Courtney raised an eyebrow. "Haven't you ever heard of a fling?"

"I've been there, done that, got the t-shirt, and took it back. Jenna Black was all about the casual fling." Lindsey swallowed some of her tea. "I don't want something quick and empty, Court. I want the fairytale, or at least the practical application of it." Courtney tipped her head in inquiry. "You know, a solid relationship based on trust, honesty, affection, and passion. A safe harbor I can retreat to and know I've found the clear water."

"You want to live on the water?"

"No, 'clear water' means to find a safe place where you have the high ground and the action is over. It's a Navy thing."

"Ahhh." Courtney nodded and a smug smile curled her lips. "I know where you can find some of that Navy clear water if you're not too scared to look for it."

Lindsey ignored the spike of hope in her gut as she leveled her friend with a flat look. "You're not going to give up on this, are you?"

"Nope."

"Court—"

"Listen, Lindsey. I've been your friend for a while now, and I know you've pushed yourself to be the best at what you do. Believe me, I've been there the whole time." She laid a hand on Lindsey's arm and squeezed gently. "But here's the thing. Everyone needs a break and burnout is right around the corner. You have leave. You have a ton of it. Go take some before you're too bogged down in cases to make it practical."

Courtney smiled and sat back, swigging her beer. "And do me a favor. Go find that SEAL and tell him you love him before you drive us all crazy."

"I do not—"

"Don't lie to me or yourself, Lindsey." Courtney held up her hand to forestall her. "I've known you long enough to know when someone has gotten under your skin, and Chief Petty Officer Andrews did it with his super secret agent skills."

"He's a SEAL, not CIA."

Courtney rolled her eyes. "Doesn't matter. They have the same sneaky-sneaky skills."

Lindsey snorted. "Sneaky-sneaky? Is that a technical term?"

"Hell, yeah." Courtney grinned and finished her beer. "Maybe you need to develop a few sneaky skills of your own and go see if smart, handsome, and sneaky is willing to be your clear water." She sobered. "Please. Do me, you, and him a favor. You deserve the chance at the fairytale you want, Lindsey. But sitting here in the damn desert won't get you any closer to it. Put in for some vacation."

"You're not my boss anymore, Court." Lindsey finished her tea and tried to swallow the dread of facing her apartment alone.

"No, I'm your friend. And I'm telling you to get a life before you implode." Courtney gave her a sympathetic look as she waved for the bill. "No one needs or deserves it more. Besides, from the outsider's perspective, I think the chief was pretty sweet on you."

Lindsey shook her head as she tossed a ten spot on the table. "How could you tell? He didn't show anything on his face or body language."

"Call it a gut feeling." Courtney's smug smile returned to her face. "You gonna go west, Jarvis?"

"This isn't some romantic movie, Court. He's probably moved on."

"So? What's the worst that can happen? You go out there and find out he's moved on. Done. Plus you'll get to see the ocean and some of those other hot SEAL men." Courtney shrugged. "Think of it this way. Nothing will happen if you don't go. But something *might* happen if you do. At least you'll get some time to recharge."

Lindsey couldn't argue with her friend. She let her gaze rest on the polished brass of the bar fixtures and ran through the scenarios in her head. *So what's it gonna be, Jarvis? Tuck tail and hide, or make your play for the brass ring?*

"I'll talk to you on Monday, Dabner."

"You gonna take leave?"

"I'll let you know." She waved as she headed for the door, her mind churning with possibilities. The question remained as to how John would respond to her just showing up.

*No, the real question is, can I handle it if he turns me down?*

****

John dropped his head under the shower spray to wash the salt water, sand, and sweat off his body. While the heat in southern California wasn't as intense as in Las Vegas, he still counted it warm enough to fry eggs on the hood of his truck. Despite the relative cool compared to the Mojave Desert, he missed Vegas.

*Correction, I miss a woman in Vegas, and the cool little cabin we shared.*

He scrubbed his body down with soap and tried to ignore his thickening cock. She'd been on his mind since he climbed into his truck and headed for the I-15, and she hadn't left it. He'd visited Coronado, learning the city and its environs, and the scents of fresh flowers and pine had him looking around for Lindsey Jarvis. Each night, he'd hit his rack with the intent to find out her new number or email address, but come morning, he'd thought better of it.

Bronco didn't really have time for a woman in his life. Not with a new duty station and a new squad to integrate with. But when he wasn't focused on the job, his mind strayed to long, dark hair and a warm, sultry voice that still came to him in dreams. God, her voice could make him come with no more than a few words.

John groaned and fisted his aching shaft, his mind full of Lindsey's sweet moans and hot mouth. He stroked himself hard and quick, not wanting to take too much time in the shower. He imagined her silken tresses sliding over his thighs as her molten, slick mouth tightened on his flesh. Pleasure and yearning overwhelmed his logical mind and his release exploded from his balls. The intensity of his orgasm couldn't compare to what he experienced with Lindsey.

Even the SEAL groupies hadn't distracted him from the woman in his memories. *I bought that damn ring. I should call her.* But the old, tired excuses came roaring back and he let the thoughts subside.

Bronco cleaned himself up and got out of the shower. He had to shake her out of his mind or call her. Except she'd gotten a new phone three weeks ago. John ignored the little voice stating he could call the Las Vegas PD directly. Hell, he could even ask for Detective Dabner if he couldn't face Jarvis. He groaned in derision as he pulled on his utilities before heading toward the mess hall for chow.

Bravo squad had just returned from a short training op to help the team and him mesh their skills. They'd finally found their rhythm and trust despite the recent loss of a squad member in Honduras. Bronco had taken the fallen man's place.

John finished his meal and headed for the squad's HQ,

his memories full of Lindsey's smile and her soft breasts against his back as she helped him through his detox. Crossing the threshold, he removed his cover and tucked it under his arm, wishing he could easily do the same to Lindsey.

*Damn, you're pathetic. Either find her or let her go.*

"Andrews."

Bronco's thoughts shattered as Lieutenant Commander Whittleton's voice intruded. John shifted direction into the commander's office.

"Yes, sir?"

"You know someone by the name of Detective Lindsey Jarvis?" Whittleton raised his eyebrows.

"Yes, sir. She was the undercover LEO who I worked with in Vegas, sir. Why?" John tried to ignore his excitement at her name.

"The front gate called. She's at the visitor's center right now asking for you. Did you leave any unfinished business in Vegas, Chief Petty Officer?"

"No, sir. Detective Dabner said the DA would be calling you, sir, and Jarvis had been moved to the sex-crimes unit. All our official business was cleared up when I left three weeks ago." But he wanted to revisit the unofficial business.

"Hmm." Whittleton eyed him carefully for a few moments. "Go see what she wants, Chief. Just remember Bravo squad is scheduled for another training at oh-four-hundred on Monday."

Bronco gaped. "Are you giving me leave for the weekend, Commander?"

"You got a problem with that, Andrews?"

"No, sir." John saluted smartly. "Thank you, sir."

"Dismissed."

Bronco retreated so fast he damn near bounced off the walls as he headed for the door. *What is she doing here? Who the fuck cares?* His thoughts ricocheted as much as his heartbeat as he caught transport to the Coronado visitor's center. He could barely hold a polite conversation with the young civilian driving and caught the muttered, "arrogant jackass" as he got out. Bronco couldn't care less. Lindsey Jarvis had come to Coronado, and he'd be damned before he wasted words on anyone before he said what he wanted to her.

John had to stop and inhale deeply a few times before enough calm filtered into his body and expression. He pulled the visitor center doors open and headed toward the information desk as he jerked his cover off his head. A school group huddled around the naval history museum, listening intently to a theatrical petty officer explaining the role of Coronado in World War II, and a few families waited in the recruitment area with their hopefuls. The young men and women looked nervous.

"Good morning, Chief Petty Officer. Can I help you?" The pretty clerk gave him a wide smile.

"Yes. I'm John Andrews. I understand I have a visitor?" He tried to keep his gaze fixed on the woman in front of him, but he kept scanning the immediate area through his peripherals.

"Let me just check. Andrews you said?"

"Yes, ma'am." Damn, a tremor ran though his body and he swore he bounced from foot to foot. Where the hell was his natural stillness and calm?

"Yes, here it is." The young woman's smile dimmed a little. "A Lindsey Jarvis is here to see you. She said she'd wait in the museum."

"Thank you, ma'am." He gave her a perfunctory smile as he shifted toward the museum, bypassing the kids oohing and ahhing over the size of the shells launched by some of the destroyers in the fleet.

The rectangular room held memorabilia from American naval warfare as far back as World War I and old black and white photos showed the variety of ships housed at the Naval base. The utilitarian carpet muffled the sound of voices, or maybe it was his pounding heart as he scanned the room full of display cases.

"Chief Petty Officer?"

He knew that contralto voice and his breath caught as he turned toward a case containing the bell musket, its lead ball shot, and a short bayonet recovered from a shipwreck off San Clemente Island. Lindsey stood beside it in a gloriously sexy sundress, fidgeting with the strap of the same purse she'd carried in Las Vegas. She'd pulled her hair up into ponytail that brushed her shoulders each time she turned her head.

"John?"

He realized he'd been staring too long and tried to find his voice to respond with some sort of coherency.

"Detective Jarvis. So nice to see you. What are you doing here in Coronado?"

Damn, could he sound any more official?

"I, uhm. Well, I came to see you. See how you're doing." She bit her lip and glanced around at the displays, trying to find her footing. She clenched her jaw before she returned her gaze to him. "You look well."

"Thanks. I am." *Kinda.* "How is the new job going for you?"

"Good. Better."

God, he hated small talk, but in the space of the public visitor's center, he found it hard to stay anything real. *Suck it up, SEAL. The only easy day was yesterday.*

"Look, I don't mean to intrude on you, Chief. I just wanted to, well, make sure you're doing okay after everything and…" She took a deep breath and straightened her shoulders, which pushed out her chest. John enjoyed the beautiful view. "See if you'd be interested in going out for coffee for real this time."

Excitement sparked in his chest and a real smile curled his lips. "That'd be great, Detective." He held out his hand.

"You can call me John."

Her smile warmed his heart as she took his hand.
"John. I'm Lindsey."

"Pleased to meet you, Lindsey. There's a great coffee
shop just off base if you'd like to go." He hadn't released
her hand yet, and he didn't want to. Just having her cherry
blossom and pine scents around him again settled some of
his restlessness.

"Yeah, that would be great."

He tugged Lindsey through the foyer and out into the
California sunshine. As soon as they stepped outside, only
the breeze and the cry of seagulls interrupted his thoughts.
He resisted the urge to bounce like a puppy after a ball as
they strode into the parking lot in silence. She unlocked the
car and he had to remind himself to let her go.

"Are you sure I'm not taking too much of your time,
John?" She bit her bottom lip and he wanted to kiss it back
to plumpness.

"Yeah, I'm sure. My CO just gave me the weekend to
take care of any unfinished business with the Las Vegas
PD, so I'm all yours, Detective." *More than you know.*

A sultry smile curled her lips and his cock saluted in
response. "That sounds great, Chief. I did have a few
questions I wanted to ask, and I recall you told me your
specialty was interrogation. Maybe you could give me a
few pointers."

"You plannin' on interrogatin' someone?" He didn't
know why that made his blood pound, but he'd happily
endure the increased pulmonary action.

"Maybe."

"Well, in that case, maybe we better go somewhere a
little more private." Preferably some place with a bedroom.
"I can't be givin' away all my secrets and techniques to just
anyone. Do you have a place to stay while you're in town?"

"I do." She raised an eyebrow as he waved to the
guards as they passed the gates of the base. "I didn't know

how I'd be received so I made sure I could at least sleep the night before I drove back to Vegas." She bit her lip again as her smile dissolved. "I didn't know if you wanted to see me after everything that happened there."

John's first impulse was to wave away her fears, but something told him he'd have better luck with honesty rather than flippancy.

"All the memories I have of Vegas with you in them are the ones I want to remember." He inhaled and flipped his heart open a little more. "I've been meaning to call you for the last three weeks, but I didn't have your number, and I didn't really know if you'd want to hear from me."

Lindsey snorted and some of the fire he loved came back. "Jeez, we're like a couple of twitchy teenagers on a first date. How old are we again?"

John laughed as the tension around them dissolved. "I'm twenty-seven last I checked. The Navy keeps pretty good records, so I'm sure it's right."

Lindsey gasped in mock horror. "Oh my goodness! I'm a cougar going for a younger man."

He raised his eyebrows. "You tellin' me you're older than me, ma'am?"

"Yep."

"How much older? Turn here. The coffee shop's around the corner."

"Guess." Lindsey grinned as they pulled into a spot at the curb.

"Oh, now, that's not fair, Lindsey. No gentleman ever tells a woman how old she is." He stepped out of the car and threw his cover on his head.

"I promise not to be offended." She smiled over the roof of her car. "If you guess right, I'll give you a prize."

The bouncing puppy sensation returned. "Can I ask a few questions first before I make my guess?"

"Sure." She winked and entered the Navy Bean Coffee Shop. John followed after like a dog on a leash. *Hey, I've been under her power since I met her.* Not a bad place to be in his estimation.

The rich scents of coffee and tea hit his nose as they stepped up to the counter. He enjoyed the play of sunlight on her hair and skin, and wished the fabric of her dress could be a little more translucent as it swished around her legs. *Get your head in the game.* He needed to be studying details of her to guess her age correctly. *She's not that much older than me.* She had the confidence of someone who'd made it to her thirties, but didn't wear the air of someone older.

"I think I'd like a short Jose Mocha." Lindsey laughed and shook her head. "I love the names of the coffee drinks here."

John reveled in her confident joy and smiled along with her. Her beauty had attracted him first, but the fire and intelligence she carried within her made him yearn for the elusive fairytale mate.

"Are you going to order, Chief Petty Officer?"

The barista's question made him jerk his attention back to coffee. "Yes, ma'am. I'll take a tall Average Joe. Black."

"Great. I'll have those ready in a bit and call you up for them. What name can I put on the order?"

"Andrews."

Lindsey allowed him to direct her to a booth beside the windows and settled herself across the table. "So, are you ready to guess?"

"No, ma'am, but I am ready to ask a few questions." Oh yeah, he was ready. Maybe he'd even slip in a few questions of a more personal nature.

"Shoot, Chief."

"Aw, now, see, that's just askin' for trouble. I'm an excellent marksman."

"Then you should be able to get the information fairly quickly, right?" Lindsey's grin charmed him. He'd never experienced the playful side of her.

"All right." The barista called out his name and he ducked to the counter to grab their drinks. He thanked her while he considered Lindsey's information a little longer as he returned to the table. "Where did you grow up?"

"All over. I was an Army brat."

"There's no accounting for taste."

"Hey now. I'm hanging out with a Navy guy." She snorted. "I figure that rounds out the military experience from an Army and Marine family a little more. They'd tell me not to waste time on swabbies."

John laughed and raised his coffee. "Touché. How long were you in the Army?"

"One tour." She sipped her coffee and grimaced.

"Not strong or rich enough?"

Her eyes widened with her grin. "Oh ho, so he does remember a few things."

"Yes, ma'am. I have a pretty good memory for details."

"Well, just remember that I like my men like I like my coffee." She winked.

"Strong and rich?" He raised an eyebrow.

"And can keep me up all night."

Bronco laughed. "I don't know about the rich part, ma'am, but the other two qualities I'm pretty good at."

"Yeah, you are." Lindsey's smile became wistful and John's mind slipped back to the times they'd shared in Vegas. Like how she looked in the morning dressed in nothing but yoga pants and a camisole. Or the glory of her riding him hard in her little black dress.

*Shit, focus on what you're supposed to be doing.* What was that again? Oh, right, guessing her age. *Mine field there, son.*

"How long have you been a cop?"

"Four years, two undercover, two as a rookie detective." She set the coffee aside and leaned back in her chair, a half smile curling her lips.

"It took two years to stop being a rookie?" John raised his eyebrows.

"When you have to learn the undercover ropes from watching rather than doing, yeah, it can take a while. And I'm a slow learner. I didn't like to screw up because it could mean my life."

"A little like the SEALs." He couldn't fault her for that. "Any college?"

"An associate's degree in management from a community college." Lindsey eyed him as he sipped his coffee and raised her chin. "How you doing there, Chief? Getting close?"

"Hey, I'm doin' recon. You can't fault a guy for gatherin' information."

She laughed and he enjoyed the sultry sound as it washed over him. Even the other men in the coffee shop turned to look for the source of the entrancing sound. He grinned.

"So, doin' some quick and dirty calculations, and taking into account your statement that you're older than me, which I'm findin' hard to believe. I'd say you're twenty-nine, and that's only because your birthday has already passed this year."

"Oh, good one, Chief. Going for the default-answer. Every older woman is twenty-nine, right?" Merriment danced in her eyes as she mock-pouted. "So close! I'm actually thirty."

John sifted through the various responses he could give, but only one thing came to mind. "I'm sorry I missed so much of those thirty years. But I'd like to take as much of the next thirty as I can."

Lindsey blinked and her laughter softened into something more serious. "What are you saying, John? And don't sugar-coat it for me. I take it straight and without dressing."

He couldn't stop the smirk curling his lips. "Yeah,

that's what I like about you." She rolled her eyes, but her smile remained intact. "I know life's uncertain. SEALs kinda wander around with that as a given. But we also figure on grabbing a good thing when we got it and if you want it straight, here it is." He met her gaze squarely. "I'd like to spend my free time with you, such that it is, getting to know the woman beneath the disguise in Vegas. I saw glimpses, and damn, you're sexy. So I'd like to learn more, Corporal Jarvis. Find out more than just how you take your coffee and how stunning you look in your little black dress."

"Now how did you know my rank in the Army?"

John grinned. "I did a little digging, Detective. I said I wanted to know you better."

Lindsey matched his smile, but her gaze skittered around the coffee shop with wary attention. "I'll tell you more, John, if you spend the weekend with me."

"Done." He didn't hesitate. If he had the chance to convince her to stay longer than the weekend, he'd take it.

She laughed. "That was easy."

"I'm a guy. I was born easy."

"I thought SEALs say, 'the only easy day was yesterday.'" Lindsey rose from her side of the booth and grabbed her purse.

"Yes, ma'am, we do, but it doesn't always apply to the members of the squad." He followed her out of the coffee shop into the sunshine, and made a quick decision as he enjoyed the hem of her skirt flirting with her legs. "Have you checked into your hotel yet?"

She tipped her head, her brow wrinkling. "No, I wanted to be sure I had a chance to see you before I told them how long I'd be staying."

"Tell you what, I just remembered a few things I'd like with me for my weekend off base, namely my car and some toiletries, and I'll meet you at your hotel. Where are you staying?" He had more than toiletries he wanted to grab, but it made a good excuse.

"The Crow's Nest Bed & Breakfast on Shoreline Street." She blushed when he whistled in appreciation. "Hey, it's my first vacation in years and I decided I deserved a little pampering."

"I'll see what I can do to accommodate you." He winked as she unlocked her car and they got in. "Just drop me at the visitor's center and I'll meet you at the B&B."

"You're not running from me, are you, John?" She raised an eyebrow as they pulled into traffic.

"No, ma'am." Far from it. He planned his next engagement. "Just want to make sure I'm prepared for anything."

She lost some of her smile. "Is that why you need your truck? So you can bolt at any time?"

"Lindsey, if I have to 'bolt at any time' it will be because that's the nature of being SpecOps, not because I want to leave you." He met her gaze steadily. "I wear my electronic leash all the time because they can call at a moment's notice." He wished he could say more to reassure her, but his plan depended upon some measure of secrecy.

"You're right. I know that, of course. I just didn't want to lose you before I'd even had a chance to get to know you better." The look she gave him warmed places in him he didn't know were cold.

"You can plan on it, Lindsey. I promise. Here, give me your new number since you got a new phone." He winked and she laughed. "I'll call you if anything comes up to change my plans. But as far as I know, my CO gave me the weekend."

She gave him the number as they returned to base and when he got out she bit her lip, uncertainty written all over her face. "See you soon?"

"Yes, ma'am. At the Crow's Nest."

She nodded and pulled away. He watched her until she drove around the corner then sought transport to Bravo

Squad's HQ, his mind already strategizing.

He'd missed Lindsey so much the first week home, he'd gone to a local jeweler and asked for a simple gold wedding band with the words "lucky charm" inscribed on the inside. But during the second week, he threw the idea of presenting her with the ring out with a reminder that they hadn't known each other long or well enough for such a gift. He'd almost pawned the ring when he'd given up on ever contacting her just this week. Her arrival on base reenergized his ideas.

His heart beat a double-time tattoo in his chest as he jumped in his truck and headed for the barracks. Now he had his chance and he'd do everything he could to make sure he never lost her again.

# CHAPTER TWELVE

Lindsey bit her lip for the hundredth time that afternoon and squeezed her cell phone in her hand. No texts or missed calls showed on the screen, even when she'd taken a shower. *No news is good news, right?* Damn, she shouldn't have let John out of her car.

Now she paced back and forth in the homey room of the Crow's Nest B&B and wondered if she'd gone completely nuts. She'd faced scarier people and places over the years undercover, but waiting for—she checked her watch—twenty-five minutes had stressed her out more than performing in front of Madame LeBeau's cameras.

*He said he'd call if he had to go to work.* Intellectually, she knew SEALs would disappear at the drop of a hat, but facing the reality before she'd even had a chance to see if a relationship would work with him in the real world sank her gut.

*Please let me convince him to give it a shot. Please give me the chance.*

Lindsey didn't put much stock in prayers, but she'd never met anyone like John Hector Andrews. He embodied her fantasy man and she'd driven all the way to Coronado for the chance to see if the fairytale could come true. *Please let me have at least a little time with him.*

All the breath left her body when her phone chirped with an incoming text. She stared at the phone, her heart thundering in her ears as she touched the screen. A blocked number showed a little envelope and her heart sank. *Oh, God, he's turning me down...*

She touched the text icon and waited for the screen to open, her stomach sinking.

*What bungalow number? Bronco*

All her breath whooshed out as she damn near slithered to the floor in relief. *He's here.* She settled for sitting on the little loveseat under the window and shakily typing in a new message with her room number. She hit send and dropped her hands to the cushions, closing her eyes. She laughed a little at herself. *God, you're pathetic.* But the relief made her giddy and she jumped when he knocked on her door.

Taking a deep breath, Lindsey couldn't help the huge grin curling her lips as she opened the door. The view on the front porch consisted of a large bouquet of red and white roses, and one grinning sailor.

"Wow."

"Sorry it took me a little longer than usual. The florist didn't have a bouquet I liked so I asked her to put one together." John extended the flowers to Lindsey. "I hope you don't hate roses."

"No, I like them. Especially when they're not from the grocery store. Those never have any scent left to them." Lindsey leaned forward to inhale the delicate fragrance curling around her. "Wow, these are extraordinary."

John stood there, gaping, and she glanced up at him in inquiry.

"Holy shit, that's so sexy."

"What is?"

"You sniffing the roses." He licked his lips and swallowed hard. "Do it again."

Lindsey laughed and inhaled again, slitting her eyes. "Did I do it right?"

"Yeah. Can I come in?"

"Absolutely." Lindsey stood back to let him pass.

He made it inside so fast the breeze lifted the ends of her hair. He dropped a duffel bag on the floor beside the loveseat before setting the roses on the little kitchenette bar. She enjoyed the roll of his ass under the butt-hugging cargo shorts as he passed and she closed the door before he could get away. *Relax, Jarvis. He showed up when he could've run. Or been deployed.*

"Thank you for the roses. They're gorgeous." She couldn't resist sniffing them again just to see the arousal darken his golden eyes.

"God, I love it when you do that." John swallowed hard as she brushed the blooms with the tips of her fingers. "Do you know why I picked red and white?"

"They smelled the best?" Lindsey inhaled again, savoring the floral scent.

"No, I just got lucky with that." He reached for her hand and held it in both of his, rubbing his thumbs over the back. "Each rose has a meaning and my mom taught me red roses mean affection and fidelity, while white roses mean truth and purity." He met her gaze and she shivered with his intensity. "You've had my affection since I met you and I'd honestly like to spend more time with you. I hope this conveys both."

"So this is the SEAL version of *semper fidalis*?"

"No, it's *this* SEAL's version of *semper fidalis*." He smiled his sexy grin. "I'm glad you showed up here to find me."

Lindsey shrugged as her face heated. "I didn't know if you'd be okay with the idea, but I couldn't stand just letting it go. Somehow we did this backwards. Sex, then dates, but I wanted to see if it was more than just sex."

"Let's see if it is. I'm game if you are." John pulled her

in close. "I want to see if it works, even if my lifestyle is a tough one for civilians to handle."

"So you're thinking long term?"

"Shhh." He nuzzled her hair and squeezed her gently. "Don't give away the plot just yet. Let's just take this weekend to learn the real us. I liked the glimpses I saw in Vegas, but the situation was less than ideal."

"Okay." Lindsey pulled back. "So what would you have done if you met me in the typical way?"

"Typical, for a SEAL?" John snorted and shook his head. "I don't think my life has much that could be called *typical*." He tipped his head with a sultry smirk. "But I want you to be a *typical* addition."

"Oh, yeah? I don't know how typical I am. Hell, you met me impersonating a psychotic man-hater. That can't be anywhere near typical." Lindsey shook her head. "But I meant if you met me in a normal place, like a bar or on the beach, or out in town, how would you have approached me?"

"You know you're asking a scary question of a guy, right?"

"Are you telling me a SEAL is afraid of asking a woman out?"

John laughed as he stepped back. "Hell, yeah. We can face down an enemy installation outnumbered and outgunned, but exposing such vulnerability as our hearts? I'm more skittish than a cat in a room full of rocking chairs."

Lindsey grinned. "So, do you want me to tell you how I'd approach you?"

"You'd ask me out?" He raised his eyebrows as he took her hand and led her toward the front door.

"Yes, I would. Where are we going?" She followed him more out of curiosity than outright agreement.

"I thought I could show you some of the cool places around Coronado I've found while we do this whole 'date' thing." He winked and waited for her to lock her bungalow door. "There's a great little seafood place, real mom-and-pop sort of thing where the owners are from the town where I grew up. I thought we could have lunch."

"Lunch sounds perfect."

He led her to his silver truck and she laughed. "I remember this truck. The first time I saw it my friend Courtney sent me a picture of it on my phone."

"The phone that you lost." He winked as he turned the ignition.

"Yes, it met with a tragic end on the edge of the bathtub."

"I think I remember hearing that."

They headed through town to the small seafood restaurant which consisted of no more than a small square building with a wraparound porch and open doors with filmy curtains. Palm trees rattled in the breeze and scents of fried food along with brackish seaweed filled the air. An older woman with short silver hair waved as soon as John stepped out of the truck.

"Welcome back, Chief. I see you've come with company this time." She winked at Lindsey as she led them to a table beneath a window with a paper window shade the same color as the curtains.

"Yes, ma'am. I believe you told me last time I shouldn't come back unless I had a friend."

"I said no such thing, Chief Andrews." Their hostess handed them menus as she admonished him with a mock-glare. "I said you need to tell more of your teammates how good my cookin' is and get them to join you when you go out." She eyed Lindsey. "This young lady is not SpecOps."

"No, ma'am, she's my date today."

Her grin bloomed immediately. "That's even better. What are you drinking?"

They gave their order and their hostess bustled away with a promise to return quickly as more customers arrived.

Lindsey watched her greet them like old friends and shook her head.

"She really knows everyone, doesn't she?"

John followed her line of sight. "Yep. Mrs. O'Neil has a special gift of knowing details about each and every repeat customer who comes in. And I swear if she could have all the single people fixed up, she'd happily do it."

"How long has she been working on you?"

"Pretty much since I walked in the door."

She laughed and he grinned. "Just like home?"

"Pretty much." John shook his head. "I think she's taken it upon herself to mother me now that she knows my mother is from the same town so far away."

Mrs. O'Neil returned with their drinks and Lindsey appreciated her subtle probing questions to determine her compatibility with John. Lindsey hoped she measured up because she wouldn't want anyone else dating him. *He's mine and has been since Vegas.* She supposed it was one trait she shared with her Jenna Black persona.

"She's not fooling around." Lindsey watched Mrs. O'Neil greet some new customers after taking their food order. "I swear she's making sure you aren't dating a dead-beat gold-digger with an eye for notching her bedpost with SEAL flesh."

John laughed. "I think you held your own and reassured her that's not who you are." He paused and raised a mock-worried eyebrow. "Are you?"

Lindsey grinned. "Nope. Besides, if I was, I'd have already notched it several times with all the stuff we did in Vegas."

"Roger that."

Their conversation shifted toward food as their meals arrived and Lindsey settled herself into enjoying the atmosphere and the company. She learned he had an older sister who married just out of high school and had three kids already, and a younger brother who escaped the "backwoods" living by going to law school and becoming a small-town lawyer.

"I think after clerking for all those big-time lawyers, he realized our small town wasn't that bad after all." John shook his head. "I'm proud of him, though. Neither of our parents had any education beyond high school, so he made a huge stride forward for our family."

"I'd say you did, too. Becoming a SEAL isn't exactly 'doing what your daddy did' in terms of default lifestyles." Lindsey sipped her lemonade and made a face at the tartness. "Plus, you've moved across the country and traveled the world for your job. Not exactly a small accomplishment."

"My mother would beg to differ. I think she'd prefer I'd stayed at home and given her grandchildren like my sister." He snorted, but his expression softened. "I don't know if children would be a good thing given my profession. Kids need a dad. Do you want kids?"

Lindsey blinked, a mixture of excitement and unease tightening her chest. "Uh…"

"Oh, sorry, that's heavy for our first real date. Just forget I asked."

"No, don't worry about it. Like you, my profession doesn't really make room for kids, and if they should have a dad, they definitely need a mom." She smiled to ease his concerns. "We were talking about family and I think mothers believe grandchildren are like currency or prestige points. My mom hasn't hinted to me that she wants them, but she might have said something to my sister."

"You haven't talked to your family yet?"

Lindsey shook her head. "Not about that. We're still trying to learn about our lives now."

"Has a lot changed?"

She shrugged. "Yeah. It's been two years and I couldn't tell them much about what I did before." She swallowed hard. "Not that I'd want them to know about the hideous world of sex slavery."

John's expression turned thoughtful. "That makes sense. Where do they live?"

"Reno. A long drive from Vegas, but still worth it."

"So you've visited them?" John grasped her hand with his, his expression hopeful.

Lindsey smiled. "Yeah. I've gone a couple of times. It was great to see my mom." The memory of her mother's face when Lindsey thanked her for the PTSD training still warmed her heart. "And Dad is good, too. I beat him at poker a couple of times."

John laughed. "Somehow that doesn't surprise me." He squeezed her hand. "Family is important. Just like teammates in the SEALs or backup as a cop. I'm glad you've reconnected with them."

"Me, too. It's all thanks to you, you know."

"Me? What did I do?"

"You reminded me of what I was missing and gave me the courage to call them after a two year hiatus." Lindsey shrugged again. "I know that doesn't make sense, but I had to thank my mom for teaching me how to help someone with PTSD. I didn't know how they'd react after so long. Picturing you regaining your strength and focus helped me find mine. It made me feel like you had my back, even if you weren't there."

John's expression softened. "I'd be happy to have your back, Lindsey. Anytime you need it."

"Thanks. That means a lot." It warmed her in ways she hadn't thought possible.

He wiped his mouth and waved for the bill. "You ready for the Coronado cool-places tour?"

"Yes, that would be great."

As John paid for lunch, Mrs. O'Neil pulled Lindsey aside with a motherly smile. "You be good to him, y'hear? That man's always alone and it isn't good for him. He needs family around him, and while I do my best, he needs someone closer than a mama."

"I'll definitely keep it in mind, Mrs. O'Neil."

The older woman eyed her keenly. "He must really like you. He hasn't brought anyone else by since he found this place three weeks ago."

*Can't imagine why that would be since you go all motherly on any potential mates.* Lindsey smiled and nodded. "I'm honored to be the first."

"Are you sassin' me?" She narrowed her eyes at Lindsey. "You think I'm just a meddling old woman, don't you?"

"No, ma'am. I think you're just watching out for single young men."

"You're right, I am." Mrs. O'Neil nodded sharply. "But the Chief, he's special. He don't have anyone out here yet, not even his squad, because he's so new. He needs someone to come home to, or he'll be lost in some of those adventures SEALs are trained to have. And he likes you enough to bring you here. Do you see what I'm saying? You're special to him and that's important. You keep that in mind."

With that final admonishment, the older woman went back to greeting her customers, offering John a wave as they left. Lindsey gritted her teeth against the woman's prying, but only because she feared she couldn't give John what he needed. *I'm only here for the weekend.* She'd have to go home to Las Vegas and couldn't be in Coronado for John. The idea made her stomach churn.

*But I want to be here for him.*

"What was all that about?" John asked as he opened her door to the truck.

Lindsey debated what to tell him while he walked around to the driver's side. She hadn't known John long, but they'd been partners in the past and trust started with honesty. She didn't have many friends she could trust, not with her previous line of work.

"She told me to be good to you because you're special, and it pissed me off because I know you're special and it's none of her damn business how our relationship goes." There. She'd said it, but she sounded petulant even to her. "I'm sorry, John. I just don't like anyone telling me to be careful when it's our job to find out about each other without someone else directing the moves." Lindsey raised her gaze to meet his. "I drove out to Coronado because I wanted to see if we could be real together, not some role we play as an undercover cop and a prisoner of the sex trade. I don't want someone telling me how to be. I just want to be myself with you."

John didn't say a word before he jerked her into his embrace and slanted his mouth over hers. Heat surged through her when his tongue demanded entrance to her lips, caressing and tangling with hers. She whimpered with relief and sensual longing, wrapping her hands in his t-shirt. Damn, this man could kiss like a pro. *This is what I want from now on.*

When he pulled back for air, he met her gaze with eyes full of warmth. "I don't want you to be anyone else with me, Lindsey. It's what I like about you." He opened his mouth to say more, but decided to brand her lips with another soul-scouring kiss before he sat back. "Let me show you my favorite places in Coronado so far."

"Okay." She wanted to say more, to solidify all the pent up emotion, but she recognized the need to let some of it go.

"If I haven't told you before, thanks for driving all the way out here to find me. I'm the jackass who didn't try hard enough to contact you." He headed back into town. "But damn, a woman who goes after what she wants is so sexy. I think I remember that from Vegas, too." He winked and she laughed as the tension bled out of the truck.

"Maybe a little."

"See? Sexy."

They toured Coronado and he showed her the best places for sunrise and sunset contemplation, his favorite ice cream shop called The Full Scoop, and a quiet, nearly deserted beach.

"I come here when I need to re-center." He stared out at the waves hissing softly over the sand. "In a squad, there isn't a lot of privacy, especially when you're new. Everyone's learning how each other works." He shrugged. "These guys have been together for at least a year and I'm new to them. It takes some adjustment."

"Not quite the well-oiled machine yet?" Lindsey nodded. It had been that way with Courtney when she started undercover work, too.

John took her hand and wove his fingers through hers as if he needed a real anchor. "We're close. We're all the best at what we do, but even so, I'm the new guy around and I gotta prove I'm good enough for their squad. I got into one of the best Teams out here on the west coast, and it's an honor, but meshing takes work."

"I bet. Do you like it?"

"What, being a SEAL?"

Lindsey snorted and thumped his shoulder with her fist. "No, being here in Coronado with this new squad. Do you like it?"

John let the silence fill in behind her words as he gazed out at the ocean. Lindsey waited for him to find whatever he wanted to say, settling into the quiet with him. Being silent and still with John filled her with contentment rather than discomfort, and any stress or fear baying at her faded into the ether. She'd never been with a man who brought out her happiness, but John did it without effort.

"I do like being here. I'm only missing one thing."

"Oh, yeah? What's that?"

"You, Lindsey." His golden gaze rested on her and her heart rate ramped up. The intensity in his eyes electrified her and her inner cheerleader turned cartwheels. "I know we haven't seen each other in three weeks, but they've been the worst three weeks since I trained with the SEALs."

"What?" Lindsey frowned. "Why?"

"Because you were still in Vegas, and when I wasn't on training or hitting the gym, or swimming laps, my mind centered on you." His lips curled in a rueful smile. "Not the best place when I had no idea if you felt the same."

"Why didn't you look me up or contact Courtney?" She snorted and shook her head. "Do you know she told me to get my ass in my car and drive out here to find you? A complete snot about it. She'd have done the happy dance if you'd called or emailed. I swear she's a romantic at heart."

John made a face then snorted. "As I said before, SEALs can face down an enemy with lots of big guns, but make us show our hearts and we run screaming like little girls."

Lindsey laughed. "This I would like to see. Big, badass SEALs running around with your hands flailing in the air, squealing."

"Yeah, not gonna happen." He grinned as he led her over to a large basalt boulder, little flecks of a green mineral catching the light of the sinking sun. "Do me a favor and sit here, please."

"Oh? What are you gonna do?"

"I'm going to stand here in the hero hour of the sun and look at you."

"Hero hour?"

"Yeah, know you, when the sun lights up a hero in the last moments of the movie to make him look majestic?" John winked. "That's hero hour."

"Ah. So all I have to do is just sit here?" She settled herself on the boulder and inhaled the warm sea air, enjoying the moisture so different from the heat of Vegas. Seagulls called overhead and their black silhouettes slid across the glowing sky. "I can look good just sitting. It's one of the few things I can do without trying."

John laughed and stood back, the sun gilding him like a bronze statue. She could stare at him as much as he could stare at her. He did look heroic with the ocean shining behind him in the rosy light. *Hero hour, indeed.*

"So, Detective Lindsey Jarvis, how would you have approached me?"

"Wow, you don't forget much, do you?"

"As I said, I have a good memory for details."

Lindsey grinned. "If I'd met you in a coffee shop in Vegas, I would have bought your coffee for you."

"Coffee shop? Not a bar?"

"Since when are bars a good place to meet people for more than just sex?"

"Friends hang out in bars." He tipped his head to the side as he shoved his hands in his pockets.

"Yep, friends or people looking for a good time, neither of which mean anything serious or romantic." She shook her head. "I'm done with quick and false. Jenna Black was all about that and she was a bitch. Thank God she was just a role I had to play. She taught me a lot about what I don't want."

Lindsey closed her eyes and tipped her head back to enjoy the sun and shoved the horrible memories away. Coronado had become a place for her to relax and start anew, not relive old pain. *And I don't want to be just friends with John Andrews.* No, she wanted more, the whole fairytale. *Hell, I rescued him like the knights of old. Don't I get to marry the prince now?* She suppressed a chuckle at the ridiculous idea.

Silence enveloped them and she wondered if John would only look at her. The waves hissed on the shore, a soothing sound playing counterpoint to the seabirds calling overhead. The sun warmed her skin, but the soft breeze dampened the heat. Some of her tension floated away and she allowed her body to relax.

"God, you're beautiful, Lindsey." John's hands brushed her thighs, the heat of them searing her skin through her skirt. "If you'd come up to me in a coffee shop, I would've asked you to join me just so I could hear your voice and look at you."

Lindsey opened her eyes when he settled between her legs, his broad shoulders pressing against her knees. "What are you doing, John?"

"Something I should've done weeks ago." He swallowed hard as he looked up at her from the sand. "Hell, I should've done it before I even got into my truck and driven away. I was a jackass."

"You're many things, Bronco, but a jackass isn't one of them." She grinned at him. "Sexy SEAL, teddy bear, great interrogator, but no jackassery evident."

He smirked, but sobered quickly. "Yeah, I was a jackass because I let go of something special. As a SEAL, I should know better than to ignore opportunities when they show up. Because they rarely show up again." He squeezed her thighs with his callused hands and pleasure zinged straight through her.

"When I met you in Vegas, I thought of you as one helluva guardian angel come to haul my ass outta the fire when you introduced yourself. Beautiful, smart, resourceful, and sexy as all get out, you charmed me like no one has before."

Lindsey snorted. "That's because I grabbed your cock and asked you to come."

John grinned. "Easiest request I've ever gotten."

She laughed.

"But even then I knew if I had the chance, I'd show you just how grateful I was to have you there." He took both her hands and met her gaze steadily. "I'd been given a lucky charm and I don't like to ignore luckily acquired charms. That's like lookin' a gift horse in the mouth."

"So, either I'm a breakfast cereal or a horse, neither is

something very complimentary." She winked and he chuckled.

"Yeah, I'm not saying this the best way, I think, but here's the deal straight." He dug out a little black box from his pocket and presented it to her. "I know we've only known each other for a little over a month and I'm a SEAL based in Coronado while you're detective in Vegas, but I also know you're the best lucky charm I've ever been given. And comin' from Vegas, that's sayin' something. So before I lose my second chance, Lindsey Jarvis, will you marry me?"

Time stopped and all sound ceased in the surge of her heart. *Wait, did he just propose?*

Lindsey blinked a couple of times before she could reach for the box with shaking hands. *Oh, my God. He just proposed.* She cracked the lid open and stared open-mouthed at the elegant flat golden band nestled in black satin. The ring sparkled in the sunshine as her joy, excitement, and elation swelled so large it escaped out her eyes in the form of liquid delight.

She squealed and threw her arms around him. "Yes!"

He laughed as he caught her and snuggled her close, his heartbeat pounding beneath her cheek on his chest. "Oh, thank you, God."

Lindsey laughed at the relief in his voice and pulled back to grin at him. His smile melted off his face when he saw her tears.

"Hey, now, are you cryin'?" He rubbed her cheeks gently with his thumbs. "What's wrong?"

She hiccoughed a laugh and shook her head. "Nothing. I'm perfect. Great." She hugged him again, trying to find some coherency. *That would happen if I wasn't so damn excited.*

"Now, you can't run away from me for long, you know." She waved the ring box at him. "This means you're mine for good, right?"

"Darlin', if screamin' and cryin' like a little girl didn't make me run, I think you're okay. And I've been yours since you showed up in that little cell in Vegas."

"I didn't scream. I squeaked with delight. Big difference."

John smirked and pulled the ring out of the box. "Let's see how this looks on your hand."

"Wait. What's that?" She turned the ring over to look on the inside. Two words had been etched along the band. "Does that say 'Lucky Charm'?"

"Yes, ma'am, 'cause you're mine." John slid the ring on her finger. "I love you, Lindsey."

She beamed, her heart expanding in her chest. "I love you, too, John. Now take me to bed and let me ride you hard, Bronco."

John barked a laugh as he hauled her off the boulder and swung her to her feet.

"Yes, ma'am."


THE END

Author's Note:

This is the prequel story in the Bad Boys of Beta Squad series. It continues with THE NAVY'S GHOST, RIMSHOT'S HARD TARGET, and BAM-BAM'S INKED HART. There is also a spin-off series call Ultimate Recon, and the first book is DARWIN'S EVOLUTION, a KindleWorlds crossover.

# THE NAVY'S GHOST
## BAD BOYS OF BETA SQUAD, BOOK 1
### SNEEK PEEK

*A SEAL is strongest with her Team…*

Ensign Christiana "Ghost" Brickman is the only female SEAL to survive BUD/S training, a real Navy Jane. But when an ambush ends her career as an active SEAL, she's free to pursue other interests. Like her two best friends Lt. Jim "Retro" Waters and Chief Warrant Officer Todd "Magic" Hunter. She's wanted them for over a year, but never dared to approach them while in the squad.

Retro has fought his dark desires since high school, certain the need to share a woman unnatural. Magic had never considered sharing before Ghost mentions it, but it solves his dilemma of choosing between his best friend and his woman. But Retro balks at Ghost's offer to share and retreats from both when she marries Magic.

Everyone feels Retro's loss, but he ignores the ache of their broken connection in favor of living 'normal.' When Ghost and the other wives of Beta Squad are kidnapped, Retro must reevaluate how much both Ghost and Magic mean to him. And he must decide how far he's willing to go to save the woman he loves, before she becomes the Navy's ghost.

# DARWIN'S EVOLUTION
## ULTIMATE RECON, BOOK 1
### SNEEK PEEK

*Sometimes retirement is a helluva lot of work...*

Retired Marine Master Sergeant Sadie Hawkins is ready for a quiet life with her mother in northern Arizona. No more recon, no more shots fired. Hell, she might even give romance a try if she finds the right guy. Like the one asleep on her shoulder on the train.

Cyrus "Darwin" Finch retired from the Navy SEALs and now runs Ultimate Recon, a security, surveillance, and rescue company employing retired members of the four branches of the U.S. military. He's on "forced" vacation and is supposed to relaxing, dammit. Until he meets Sadie.

When they discover a foreign enemy setting up a domestic retreat in Sadie's backyard, romance and vacations take a backseat. There are no calm seas or clear skies with bullets flying, and no time for a Happy Ever After. But SEALs never give up and Marines never surrender.

# OTHER BOOKS BY SIOBHAN MUIR

Queen Bitch of the Callowwood Pack (from Siren blishing)
Not a Dragon's Standard Virgin (from Siren Publishing)

Cloudburst Colorado Series
*A Hell Hound's Fire* (from Three Lakes Books)
*The Beltane Witch* (from Three Lakes Books)
*Christmas I.C.E. Magic* (Happy Holidays from the
Crescent Moon Lodge Anthology)
*Cloudburst Ice Magic* (from Three Lakes Books)

Rifts Series
*Take the Reins* (from Three Lakes Books)
*A Centaur's Solstice Wish* (from Three Lakes Books)

Bad Boys of Beta Squad Series
*Bronco's Rough Ride* (from Three Lakes Books)
*The Navy's Ghost* (from Three Lakes Books)
*Rimshot's Hard Target* (KindleWorlds Crossover)
*Bam-Bam's Inked Hart* (from Three Lakes Books)

The Ivory Road
*A Walk in the Sand* (from Three Lakes Books)
*Outback Dreams* (from Three Lakes Books)

Current Stand-alones
*Order of the Dragon* (Warbler Peninsula #1)
*Second Chance Succubus* (Capitol of Second Chances #1)
*Darwin's Evolution* (KindleWorlds Crossover)
*Her Devoted Vampire* (from Three Lakes Books)

**Coming Soon**
*Rope a Falling Star*
*The Valkyrie's Sword* (Warbler Peninsula #2)

# ABOUT THE AUTHOR

Siobhan Muir lives in Cheyenne, Wyoming, with her husband, two daughters, and a vegetarian cat she swears is a shape-shifter, though he's never shifted when she can see him. When not writing, she can be found looking down a microscope at fossil fox teeth, pursuing her other love, paleontology. An avid reader of science fiction/fantasy, her husband gave her a paranormal romance for Christmas one year, and she was hooked for good.

In previous lives, Siobhan has been an actor at the Colorado Renaissance Festival, a field geologist in the Aleutian Islands, and restored inter-planetary imagery at the USGS. She's hiked to the top of Mount St. Helens and to the bottom of Meteor Crater.

Siobhan writes kick-ass adventure with hot sex for men and women to enjoy. She believes in happily ever after, redemption, and communication, all of which you will find in her paranormal romance stories.

Connect with Siobhan online at:
http://siobhanmuir.com
http://www.facebook.com/siobhan.muir.35
http://www.tsu.co/SiobhanMuir
http://twitter.com/SiobhanMuir
http://siobhanmuir.blogspot.com
http://pinterest.com/siobhanmuir.35